Why Britain Needs Our Monarchy

Never Again To Be Taken For Granted

Why Britain Needs Our Monarchy

Never Again To Be Taken For Granted

Bob Whittington and Kartar Lalvani

Amazon Publishing

First published in Great Britain in 2023

ISBN-978-1-916540-75-0

"We may have been reminded how much of her presence and contribution to our national identity we took for granted."

-HRH The Princess Royal
Her personal tribute to HM Queen Elizabeth II

Personal address by

HM King Charles III

On Christmas Day, 2022

"And at this time of great hardship - be it for those around the world facing conflict, famine or natural disaster, or for those at home finding ways to pay their bills and keep their families fed and warm - we see it in the humanity of people throughout our nations and the Commonwealth who so readily respond to the plight of others."

"... whatever faith you have, or whether you have none... I believe we can find hope for the future."

"My mother's belief in the power of that light was an essential part of her faith in God, but also her faith in people- and it is one which I share with my whole heart. It is a belief in the extraordinary ability of each person to touch, with goodness and compassion, the lives of others and to shine a light in the world around them. This is the essence of our community and the foundation of our society."

CONTENTS

Preface   XI

Introduction   XVI

Our Royal Family   1

Our History   33

Our Democracy   49

Our Judiciary   65

Our Military   74

Our Police   93

Our NHS   101

Our Freedom of Belief   114

Our Education   125

Our English Language   138

Our Benign Climate   150

Our People   160

The Commonwealth   173

Our United Kingdom   186

Epilogue   201

Postscript   209

About the Authors   2

Preface

"Rights Triumphing Over Responsibilities"

Serendipity was the catalyst for writing this short book. By chance we detected a mood in the country which coincided with Her Majesty Queen Elizabeth's Platinum Jubilee celebrations.

The mood was a curious mixture of universal joy at her outstanding achievement, a momentous occasion which was recognised the world over, combined with a reluctance to accept what a lucky realm we live in with a history of endeavour which could never be equalled.

Everyone, it seemed to us, is too quick to moan, too ready to demonstrate their anger at the slightest offence and an unwillingness to recognise that, without the solid foundations which the United Kingdom has built up over the centuries, life could be very different. It has become a land of rights triumphing over responsibilities.

By focusing on the treasures, the positives, for just a brief moment, it was obvious to us that the bounties we are blessed with far outweighed the negatives. At the same time, we acknowledge the flaws and the errors of the past which were a reflection of their time. We acknowledge the flaws of the present, the economic tensions, the dangers of war, the social unrest, but then we ask which other nation does not have similar challenges, or even worse.

Importantly we challenge all to look at ourselves in the mirror and ask what we could be doing to help ourselves, to keep healthy for example and thus ease the burden on an overstretched NHS.

Shouldn't we try first to understand the history of our land, its benefactors and its leaders before we leap to condemn everything about our past which does not fit in with our sanitised, politically correct and narrow-minded view of the world, and worse deny others the right to an alternative point of view?

What we wondered would have become of so many different countries without the existence of the British Empire, was it all so bad that we should never have introduced our industrial expertise, our democratic ways and even our language? Kartar Lalvani identifies a parallel with the success of India which has thrived through its development as part of the British Empire and which today so many seek to disparage. There were certainly flaws in British rule but so much more was achieved during those 200 years.

Now we want to abandon all that has made us strong, a pillar of the western world, a united nation which attracts visitors and immigrants from around the world to admire what they see, to study at our universities and to settle. Some argue that it would be better to break up our country, that they would be better off alone, but that is not the experience of countries making up the Commonwealth which have chosen to become independent sovereign nations but to remain permanent members of the association with the British monarch as its head, stronger together.

So why, we wondered, do we not leap to the defence of our Monarchy? Why, particularly in the early months of 2023 as the. coronation of King Charles approached, were there so many critics of a system which has served us well over the centuries and why were more loyal citizens not answering back to denounce the half-truths, malicious innuendo and personal abuse? We believe the time is right to take a greater pride in a land which is indeed gratefully and proudly our own and, therefore, have a duty of care to denounce those critics who at the lowest level simply moan, but also others who have more sinister motives, bent on denigrating the jewels which combine to make our United Kingdom so precious. It is easy to criticise from the side-lines, it is harder to take to the field and defend with all one's might against the republican arrows of prejudice and malice. Furthermore, we have refrained from countering these attacks with our own out of courtesy and discretion.

Far from being irrelevant, our monarchy provides a constancy and leadership as we will demonstrate, and we have a monarch who, as Prince of Wales, fearlessly challenged convention and championed causes which belatedly others have chosen to follow. Where else in the world can one find such historical solidity and leadership? Where else would one find a head of state who has a duty to serve without the ability to defend, to act as a figurehead in times of struggle without the constitutional right to speak out forthrightly and voice an opinion when all around others choose to snipe and sneer?

We could all do well to take a leaf out of the example set so long ago by Her Majesty Elizabeth II when she vowed to dedicate her life to serving her people which she did for decades without so much as a murmur of complaint when things went gone wrong for herself or her family.

Kartar Lalvani and Bob Whittington

Introduction

What has become of our country, this United Kingdom, where we choose to attack everything that has made us strong, a nation with a history without parallel and at its head we have a Monarchy revered around the world. Revered that is except, it seems, among its own people.

The king may be our head of state, but he and his family have a duty to serve. One might even say that they are prisoners within their own castle not free to enjoy the wealth which surrounds them like billionaire maharajahs, but as custodians of their unique inheritance.

They are cursed by an inability to speak up in their own defence, their children who many see as pampered, are just as trapped, trained from birth to live a life of service, never to answer back. The discipline they must endure is surely the toughest apprenticeship in any walk of life. The whole family must smile, regardless of the barbs which are thrown in their path to ensnare them – many of which come from a startling direction.

Today we have a king, who as Prince of Wales, was a pioneer in so many different fields from the environment, to architecture, to healthcare. But at a stroke, with the sad death of his mother, HM Queen Elizabeth, he is now on that same pedestal and the world is watching, while some wish him to fall, daring him to speak his mind which now he cannot.

Queen Elizabeth served us for seven decades and earned our respect and love, but with astonishing speed the mood has changed as republicans gather confidence to challenge an established order of things because she is no longer there. There is a certain cowardice at such a personal assault which ill becomes our land, and what is the purpose, what is the motive?

It is clear that it is driven by a desire to destroy the monarchy which has been weakened not only by the death of HM Elizabeth but by self-inflicted fire from within. Those who by instinct are anti-monarchist seize on these moments like vultures hovering round a weakened prey. They must not succeed because the very fabric of our society will suffer as we will demonstrate in the following chapters.

We should instead be counting our blessings that we live in a constitutional monarchy and not some totalitarian state or under the crushing fist of a dictatorship. Increasingly we are quick to condemn without pausing for a moment to appreciate what we have and what others envy.

The monarchy is a gift to be treasured not something to be squandered or abused, particularly when it looks vulnerable because, should it ever disappeared, its magic can never be recaptured. And that is not the magic of some fairy tale, it is the magical history which has served this land for centuries, always moving with the times, adapting and serving; leading charitable causes in their thousands or shining a light on forgotten and shunned sectors of societies, such as AIDs sufferers or the victims of landmines. What, we ask, would replace it? A politician can be a president for a time but only as long as they can keep the support of voters. A king ascends to the throne, yes by accident of birth, but also by having served that apprenticeship which prepares him to be nothing grander than a servant of his people.

And what is the reward, a comfortable home to live in and a car to drive? Definitely, but also never-ending thankless duties to perform, speeches to make, people to greet? And now, in these days of anger and envy, a torrent of abuse to be withstood in silence.

Why Britain Needs Our Monarchy is not a journey through a nation's history with rose-tinted glasses. It is written at a time of economic crisis which spared no household and challenged businesses to survive. There should be no denying it, the very monarchy is under threat too.

Conflicting predictions were made about how long the economic hardship was likely to endure, some suggesting recession lasting into 2026, while others forecasting that once stockpiles of gas, oil and wheat were replenished, prices would stabilise. Time will tell. However, what this book does is seek to restore the balance of injustice and to appreciate what is on the other side of the coin before our history and our way of life and our constitutional monarchy are rewritten with the poisoned pen of anger, jealousy and prejudice. It is intended to appeal to those with an open mind and a keen interest in a country which throughout the centuries has absorbed and benefitted from its visitors and even its invaders, and whose spirit resolutely refuses to be crushed.

We live in a world where the emphasis is on criticising at the expense of appreciating anything that is good and worth preserving, or at the very least worth recognising for the benefits that an institution or a heritage has delivered. And the easiest target of all is a king and his family who must depend on right thinking, loyal people to rush to their defence.

This book unashamedly seeks to champion the achievements of a unique constitutional monarchy, British endeavour, systems and organisations which do their best for us because the world is determined to find fault wherever possible while pretending that there is nothing to uphold as even a little worthwhile. It's a reminder to pause occasionally to take stock of our bounties as we rush headlong into embracing the latest destructive campaigns fanned by the indiscriminate winds of the Internet. We discount our history as irrelevant because it is old and out of date without considering that it has something to teach us. Some want to disband the monarchy and turn their homes into museums.

Our colonial history, the days of the Raj, is often picked on to denigrate what has happened in the past, but in those 200 years what was achieved for a great new nation of India, divided among some 670 maharajahs and hundreds of disparate states, in a land where some 20 languages were spoken, is astonishing. Indeed, in the early 18th century the country was so divided and corrupt that the much-reviled East India Company (EIC) could not fail to bring order. Of the corruption he witnessed, Robert Clive wrote to his fellow directors of the EIC in London: "I can assert with some degree of confidence that this rich and flourishing kingdom may be totally subdued by so small a force as 2000 Europeans." A single language, English, brought unity of commerce and governance, a single authority brought peace among countless mini-rulers, and engineering feats of such magnitude were achieved that they will never be equalled. The list of accomplishments is staggering: the establishment of the first universities in Bombay, Calcutta and Madras (there were 17 by the time the British left), the shipbuilding industry, the ports, the steel industry, the construction of thousands of miles of railway lines and more than 175,000 railway bridges helping to unify the country, workshops, canal and water systems, and the creation of a professional and unified army to mention just a few. The list in short is endless. Kartar Lalvani challenges anyone to argue with his contention that **the 200 years of British rule in India were the most progressive two centuries in the country's last 1,000 years.** They rendered to India progressive and scientific governance, including creation of an esteemed Indian Civil Service, an independent judiciary with trained judges, directly elected central and state assemblies and provincial self-government. In time, of course, India was ready for self-rule and has never looked back, its own politicians and entrepreneurs rising to prominence and, in modern times, its brightest sons and daughters coming to Britain to create futures of their own. It was that astounding blend of commercialism, at times exploitative, and high-minded liberalism which mixed so well with the Indian culture. Perhaps, what is equally astonishing, is that seldom, if ever, does one hear a voice raised in praise of what Britain achieved in those 200 years, rather the criticism is deafening. Where is that British characteristic of restraint and moderation when it comes to denouncing the British way? Well, never again.

And yet with such a history, we are moaners, obsessed with our rights and forget our personal responsibilities, we are too ready to blame and too slow to understand and to forgive, too loud in our opinions and too unwilling to listen. Those who have known real hardship in other lands call it "the British disease" – nothing is ever good enough, nothing will satisfy.

Why Britain Needs Our Monarchy is a bold defence of the realm. It is a celebration of all that is British, and all that should be cherished about a small island nation with a remarkable history. Nothing and no-one are without flaws, but that should never be a reason to disown or abuse everything else that is good. Why Britain Needs Our Monarchy accepts those flaws but seeks to highlight what Great Britain has achieved.

We have given a language, a democratic system, jurisprudence and so much more to the world, and in return many of the peoples we have ruled over during those Imperial days have sent their sons and daughters to live and work here. According to accountants, Grant Thornton, London is the preferred location for more than half of the 63 fastest growing Indian companies. (India Meets Britain Tracker, 2019).

We have demonstrated how a monarchy can be sustained and thrive when the alternatives look less flexible, perhaps even threatening, and our customs and way of life have been a magnet to refugees fleeing conflict and famine, and economic migrants who just want a better life and preferably one with free benefits. There must be a reason why so many of the people risking all in the Channel on a flimsy craft haven't bothered to stay in other countries that they have had to cross first, which pose absolutely no threat to them. 43,665 migrants applied for asylum in the UK in 2021 according to the UN's Refugee Agency, making it the highest number of asylum claims since 2004.

Why Britain Needs Our Monarchy is intended to appeal to those with an open mind and a keen interest in a country which throughout the centuries has absorbed and benefitted from its visitors and even its invaders, and whose spirit resolutely refuses to be crushed.

Just days before the coronation of King Charles, a BBC poll showed that more than a third of Generation Z (18-24 year olds) want the monarchy to be abolished. Instead, they would prefer an elected head of state. (BBC Panorama 24 April 2023).

On the other hand, the majority of adults (78%) give their wholehearted support to the crown and would view the trend among young people with anguish and no little anger. We set out in the following pages why the younger generation are mistaken and why they should cherish the finest of British institutions which has no parallel in history.

The BBC poll draws attention to the <u>perceived wealth</u> of the royal family in the eyes of the young which, of course, is a wholly mistaken concept as we will underscore. They are not billionaires, they are custodians

of their position and their inheritance for future generations, and for the benefit of the nation.

But the monarchy, the king and his family, can give no answer. In a nation famous for upholding basic human rights, others must answer for them, putting the arguments forcefully and challenge an increasingly vocal opposition to present a compelling alternative if they have one.

Today we have a monarch who has lived his life championing causes in the national interest he holds dear and now, as king, his role is greater still, to serve his people to the end of his life. Long may he reign and never again to be taken for granted.

Kartar Lalvani and Bob Whittington

Our Royal Family

'Stability, Continuity and Service"

As HRH The Prince Philip used to say: "We are first and foremost a family not a secret society." He was referring, of course, to his immediate family, his wife, Queen Elizabeth II, and their four children, and just like any family they have their highs and lows, but unlike any family they are constantly in the public eye, and therefore easy targets rarely able, nor willing, to answer back.

The British royal family has been continuously evolving, alert to changing times, while preserving what makes the "Firm" a unique institution. But the public is demanding, give a little and we want more, more access, more right to comment and criticise, and we forget what a treasure we have. It is taken for granted that we live in a monarchy, but if that demands just a little deference then we ask why. Why do they live in palaces, surrounded by luxury and privilege, why should we pay for all this 'bling' when so many are going hungry, struggling to make ends meet?

Those who demand the abolition of the monarchy are well within their rights, but what alternative are they proposing: a presidential system, a republic, a dictatorship? We tried it once, as every schoolchild knows, when Oliver Cromwell, a leading figure demanding the execution of King Charles I in 1649, established The Protectorate. He ruled as Lord Protector over the Commonwealth of England, Scotland and Ireland between December 1653 until his own death in September 1658. The Protectorate did nothing for democracy. "Cromwell quickly tired of his own first parliament which suddenly began to have second thoughts about all the power they had bestowed upon him. His first solution was to use his soldiers to bar any member who refused to agree to his terms and finally, as the debating continued, he dissolved the parliament in January 1655, it having failed to enact a single law."[1] King Charles II then became king in 1660 with the Restoration of the Monarchy, and we have enjoyed the stability of a monarchy ever since. Is it better to live in a world where change is constant or where there is underlying continuity? Sometimes

---

[1] Money Talks – British Monarchs and History in Coins, Bob Whittington (*Whittles Publishing, 2017*)

change can be brutal, sometimes for good and sometimes for ill. Take a look, for example, at life in the days before Rhodesia, once dubbed "the Jewel of Africa", declared independence and became Zimbabwe under Robert Mugabe and ask ourselves how the country benefitted thereafter. Or what happened to Iran's economy after the expulsion of the Shah in 1979? Was Egypt a stronger nation when Gamal Abdel Nasser and a group of army officers overthrew King Farouk in the 23 July Revolution 1952 bent on abolishing the constitutional monarchy and establishing a republic? King Farouk famously remarked: "In 100 years' time, there will only be five kings left: the king of hearts, clubs, diamonds and spades and the king of England."

The royal line of succession in Great Britain offers a constancy that other nations can only envy. Of course, there were battles, there was even regicide and that short spell as a "Commonwealth and Protectorate", but as the United Kingdom of Great Britain and Northern Ireland today it offers a welcome stability in a world where there is anything but. Queen Elizabeth could trace her ancestry back to Queen Victoria, her great, great grandmother, and beyond that to Alfred The Great, king of the West Saxons (871-886). It is that remarkable line of succession which set her and her family apart from every other monarch and world leader. Indeed, by 2022 she had become the longest reigning monarch and the longest serving incumbent head of state. Fifteen British prime ministers had served under her since she ascended the throne on 6 February 1952 at the age of 25, which meant she had a wealth of political experience on which to draw, and to advise.

It is this stability and continuity which has lasted for centuries since the first Anglo-Saxon kings and upon which this island nation is built. It was tribal at first, piecemeal, but ultimately durable, and became the United Kingdom in 1800 when the parliaments of Great Britain and Ireland passed the Act of Union creating the United Kingdom of Great Britain and Ireland. Nearly a hundred years earlier in 1707 by a previous Act of Union the United Kingdom of Great Britain was established when Scotland gave up its parliament, but not its distinct legal system based on Roman Law, unlike the law of England and Wales based on Case Law, statute and convention.

Today there is, of course, a concerted effort to divide the UK, going beyond the devolved administrations, with Scottish figures campaigning for an independent Scotland; and Welsh nationalists pursuing similar aims. And with the victory of Sinn Fein in Northern Ireland in the May 2022 elections, there was renewed talk of one united Ireland. But Queen Elizabeth seemed to have pre-empted this when she addressed the Houses of Parliament marking her Silver Jubilee in May 1977:

"I cannot forget that I was crowned queen of the United Kingdom of Great Britain and Northern Ireland", adding: "Perhaps this jubilee is the time to remind ourselves of the benefits which union has conferred at home and in our international dealings, on the inhabitants of all parts of this United Kingdom." As Michael Cole, the former BBC royal correspondent, wrote: "It was in code, but her meaning was clear. The queen was warning her legislators that if they messed about with her realm, they would have to do it without her." (*Sunday Express,* 14 May 2022). A delicate example also of how the Queen exerted "soft power" long before the term was coined.

This may not be the place to rehearse the arguments for and against the monarchy, but it is fair to challenge the wisdom of destroying an established entity which has stood the test of time. We are most certainly in danger of taking for granted its benefits without the certainty of what such a schism might offer.

The British Monarchy is a robust institution. And yet it seems fragile and endangered, entering stormy and uncharted waters. For more than seventy years the Queen steadied the ship. She had an outstanding record of dutiful service and even the diehard republicans had for the most part spoken no ill of her, since it would have damaged their cause and there was no ill to be spoken.

Until that is Harry and Meghan chose to fire shots in their Netflix series at her legacy, attacking the Commonwealth as Empire 2, carefully editing Her Majesty's own speeches to suit their Imperial agenda[2], as well as ill-disguised slights against his own family. Earlier, republicans had reserved their attacks for other members of her family who have obligingly presented themselves as easier targets. One of their billboards showed a life-size image of Prince Andrew with the slogan 'No one is above the law.' But nothing is for ever, not even the reign of our longest serving and longest living monarch. However, it is worth setting out the benefits that we derive from this unique and British way of doing things. If we lose them, we shall surely regret it.

The essence of the case lies not only in the merits of the monarchy but also in the demerits of the alternative, both in what we have and in what we stand to lose. Both are palpable and evident – except of course to the blind-sided republicans, who with Her Majesty's passing see a new opportunity to call for change despite most polls remaining stubbornly in favour of the monarchy.

---

[2] On her 21st birthday Her Majesty said: "I declare before you all that my whole life, whether it be long or short, shall be devoted to your service and the service of our great imperial family to which we all belong." In the edited version it has been cut to: "I declare before you all that my whole life, whether it be long or short, shall be devoted to the service of our great imperial family to which we all belong."

The first benefit is that the monarch is above and beyond party politics. The monarch reigns but does not rule. He does not even vote or carry a passport. The government of whatever colour is his government and governs the country in his name. No parliamentary bill becomes law until he gives his assent to it. Nor is it conceivable that he would refuse his consent (except perhaps to a bill to abolish the monarchy). The House of Commons, though it represents the people, actually sits in a royal palace, the Palace of Westminster. The state opening of Parliament is a classic compromise between the ceremonial and the functional. He proclaims the government's policies to Parliament in his speech in the House of Lords, read but not written by himself, whether or not he agrees with them. Apart from the Speaker's procession in the House of Commons and a few other fripperies involving wigs and gowns and maces, pomp and power are kept with a firewall between them. We have no need for a written constitution when the head of state and head of government are so serendipitously separated. The separation is understood and does not need to be argued about. The only grey area between them is the extent to which his government should heed his advice; but a Prime Minister of any party would be foolish to ignore it.

The power of the political parties has increased, is increasing and ought to be diminished. It would be increased still further, and most damagingly, by the politicisation of the role of head of state.

The advantage of the present arrangement is its resilience. Governments rise and fall. They are popular or unpopular. They are voted in and voted out. They will disappoint but they should not betray. They make mistakes – for example, in recent times, embarking on an unwinnable war in Iraq on the basis of false intelligence, and on another unwinnable war in Afghanistan in defiance of all the lessons of history. But these are not the mistakes of the head of state. Although carried out in Queen Elizabeth's name at the. time and by her armed forces, she was not responsible for them, and remained untarnished by them. An elected political head of state would carry baggage from causes that he or she had previously supported and would have to bear the consequences.

And once a year, at the Cenotaph on Memorial Sunday, the monarch attends a ceremony in honour of those who died in conflicts entered into by their politicians and those of their predecessors. It may ease the grief of the bereaved to reflect that their loved one died for Queen, or King, and country rather than for the Secretary of State for Defence or the Minister for the Armed Forces. 457 of them were sacrificed in Afghanistan, mostly in Helmand Province between 2001 and 2021, to no one's benefit or advantage. The policy, such as it was, was entered into by one government and continued by the next, until finally being abandoned in defeat.

Now imagine the election of a republican president of the United Kingdom, or Lord Protector in its previous incarnation. First there would be a dispute about whether his or her election should be done by the popular vote or by the elected representatives in Parliament. Australians were divided on this in 1999 and it resulted in an unexpected defeat for the republicans. Then the toxins of party politics would take over. There is no way that the parties could keep their hands off it. The prize would be just too glittering, not only to keep it for themselves but to deny it to the others and all the patronage that would go with it; never underestimate the power of the negative in deciding the course of elections.

The interested parties would want their own candidate to occupy the throne, or the dais, or the saluting base, or the quarterdeck, or wherever the seat of ceremonial power might be. They would not trust any of their rivals not to abuse that power but by the same token would have no hesitation in abusing it themselves. They would denigrate the other candidates by the pejorative campaigning, which is a feature of all elections, including the presidential. Their own man or woman would be equally damaged before taking office. By doing so, even with the best of intentions, they would demean the office that they were trying to seize. It is a system of democratic appointment that may suit other countries, like the Republics of Ireland and France, but emphatically would not suit ours.

In ours the transfer of power is assured, within a single family, from one of its members to another in the order of their birth. (The law was changed in 2011, with the consent of all the Queen's realms, to allow equal rights of succession to females as well as males in the Royal Family.) The transfer has not always been smooth, and there have been usurpations along the way well chronicled by William Shakespeare. Our disputed successions go back to the Wars of the Roses, between the houses of Lancaster and York, but they ended on Bosworth field in 1485. Richard III was the last English monarch to die in battle. T.S. Eliot then believed he was also the last truly legitimate King of England. There were always doubts about the legitimacy of foreign monarchs, especially the Hanoverians.

The House of Windsor, by contrast, is challenged in its second century by no other dynasty. The outcome is an oasis of calm in a turbulent world. We would be wise to hold on to it. Walter Bagehot, the Victorian essayist, wrote of a different Queen: 'The best way of testing what we owe to the Queen is to make a vigorous effort of the imagination and see how we should get on without her...A monarch that can be truly revered, a House of Peers that can be truly respected, are historical accidents nearly peculiar to this island, and entirely peculiar to Europe.' [*The English Constitution*, Oxford University Press 2001, p.55.]

And history shows us that the existence of the monarchy is no impediment to parliamentary reform, to which the King or Queen has invariably assented, even if like King William IV and Queen Adelaide in 1832 they were personally opposed to it. What they did not know, but their successors discovered, was that reform was in the monarchy's best interest.

The second benefit connects with the first in the matter of stability. The monarchy is an antidote to extremism. The thought occurs: we do not have military *coups* in our country, although there were rumours of one during the premiership of Harold Wilson. The steadying influence of the monarchy has something to do with it. Our last military *coup* was the one that overthrew the post-Cromwell regime in 1660, when General George Monck, 1st Duke of Albemarle, marched his army south from Scotland. The armed forces are non-political. They pledge their allegiance not to the government of the day but to the Crown. Each regiment has a member of the royal family as its Colonel-in-chief. When regime change occurs, it is through the ballot box and not through an uprising of the military. Thus, it can be argued that, paradoxically, our monarchy is actually a buttress of our democracy. The monarchy is a peculiar institution, and this is one of its evident advantages.

The royal Colonels-in-chief could not easily be replaced by the relatives of an elected ex-politician. The regiments would simply not agree to it. We could expect an exodus of senior officers, and (just as important) of regimental sergeant-majors, the backbone of the Army, who would rather resign than pledge their allegiance to a political head of state.

The third benefit is to enable the United Kingdom to occupy a place in the world beyond its ability to project hard or soft power. The diplomats used to express this as 'punching beyond our weight', a phrase by now outdated and discredited. Yet we still retain, in two respects, the trappings of what we were when we possessed the furthest flung empire that the world has ever known. One of these is a permanent seat on the Security Council of the United Nations; it includes the power of veto and the responsibilities that go with it. The other is the monarchy itself, with for 70 years a widely admired and long-serving monarch at the head of it. The power balance has shifted between the old world and the new, and the 'special relationship' between the United Kingdom and the United States no longer reflects its reality, indeed it is a term seldom used by the Americans themselves. But American Presidents - even in his time the showman Donald Trump – have craved their invitations to Buckingham Palace or Windsor Castle. It is a privilege that campaign funds cannot buy and the destination of choice for a President on his first overseas tour. This applies both to Republicans and Democrats - to Donald Trump and Joe Biden, the one of German and the other of Irish origin. The only absentee was Lyndon Johnson – and that had something to do with a foreign war. The British stayed away from Vietnam, and he stayed away from the Palace.

The fourth benefit is economic and impossible to quantify. The British monarchy is the best known and, in some respects, most spectacular in the world. At least before the pandemic, it drew millions of visitors to these shores to marvel at the palaces and the pageantry, the military ceremonies, the Changing of the Guard, the pride and plumage of the Royal Knights of the Garter, the Yeomen of the Guard and all the rest of the royal cavalcade. The state opening of Parliament is the British equivalent of a joint session of the US Congress. It features not only the monarch but their courtiers, the Gold Stick-in-Waiting, the Silver Stick-in-Waiting, the Adjutant Silver Stick-in-Waiting and others whose titles and functions, mostly as bodyguards to the monarch, date back to the Middle Ages. Add to those the Hereditary Grand Falconer and the Ravenmaster of the Tower of London. We would be a poorer country without them, both culturally and financially. They also provide colourful and secure employment to the old soldiers of the Yeomen of the Guard. By way of contrast, the souvenir sellers could expect slim pickings from the election and inauguration of President First-past-the-post.

The fifth benefit is that the existence of the monarchy dignifies and moderates the honours system. It is right that people are honoured for their services to the community. It is not right at all that those being honoured are being rewarded for large donations to political parties. The citations refer to their 'public and political services'. The British Empire no longer exists, except in its CBEs, OBEs and MBEs. These could be changed without difficulty to the Order of British Excellence, if it was felt to be necessary, since the British Empire is somewhat out of fashion.

There are questions to be asked of the republicans, should they prevail. If Scotland were to break away from the Union, would it have its own republican head of state? (The Scottish National Party has a republican wing within it and is power sharing with the Scottish Greens who are also republican.) And likewise, Wales? And what of Northern Ireland, historically the most divided of our four nations? The patrons of the many hundreds of charities in which the royals are involved could, of course, be replaced by commoners without difficulty but with regret. The President's family would not be populous enough to provide enough of them; and besides, it would keep changing every few years. The national anthem has a more than adequate substitute standing by, in Hubert Parry's *Jerusalem*. The alternative, Elgar's *Land of Hope and Glory*, is probably ruled out by its nostalgia for the Empire.

Next, what of the regiments and military formations of which the Princes and Dukes are Colonels-in-chief? Of the very names of the Royal Navy, Royal Marines and Royal Air Force? Or the future of the Trident submarine base at Faslane? Would the former royal palaces become places of republican pilgrimage? Would the Royal Albert Hall become the People's Palace? And the Royal Philharmonic Orchestra the Orchestra of the People's Republic? The Royal Society for the Protection of Birds could redistribute the lettering and become the SPRB, the Society for the Protection of Republican Birds. The multiple re-namings would themselves be divisive and disputatious, even if the Union stayed together – and one of the forces that keeps it together is a shared allegiance to the Crown. The four nations of the United Kingdom have more than enough divisions among them and within them already to have another one gratuitously added to them.

The colourful thread of monarchy that runs through the nation is often hardly noticed because we have always lived with it and it is part of the daily texture of our lives. Our government and opposition are His Majesty's. Our post boxes bear the royal initials. Our Lifeboat Institution is Royal (even in Ireland it is Royal). Our judges sit in the Royal Courts of Justice. Our criminals serve their sentences at their Majesty's pleasure and in their Majesty's Prisons. We pay our taxes to their Majesty's Customs and Revenue. Monarchy or monochrome? That is the question to be decided, even before we get around to debating whose head should be on the banknotes and the coinage; and at what cost and how often they should be changed.

There is also the matter of history and continuity which are woven into the narrative. We are who we are, in part at least, because we were who we were. The royal succession has not been a smooth-running river, but a waterway set about with perilous shoals and rapids: it has passed from one family to another, sometimes under dubious circumstances and by force of arms; it has been broken completely and briefly in the seventeenth century, and at one point been more German than British. George II was simultaneously the Elector of Hanover, preferred to live there and spoke to his ministers in French.

But today's monarchy is ours and no one else's except for the King's other realms. It adorns our sense of identity with a human face. It binds our past to our present and our present to our future. We are, except for a vociferous minority, at ease with it. We are privileged to have inherited it. It is our succession as well as theirs. It is part of who we are. Legions of foreigners envy us because we have it and would like to have one of their own, rather than be presided over by a former political grafter. It will probably, but not necessarily, survive because it is more attractive than the republican alternative. But it will not survive unaided and on its own by the divine right of its kings and queens. No such thing exists in the twenty-first century. We are so much better off with it than without it. We will do well to support it, loyally and steadfastly and courteously, long to reign over us.

The royal family represents the whole nation – England, Scotland, Wales and Northern Ireland. When, as a young man, Prince Charles was presented to the people of Wales as their prince at his investiture in 1969, it was to cement those ties; it was not a case of ownership, it was a symbol of service, in the same way as the Queen was Head of the Commonwealth, not to rule but to serve. In any case, there were said to be no plans for a lavish investiture ceremony for Prince William as his father had when he was 20 at Caernarfon Castle, instead William and Kate would be "taking time to strengthen their relationship with communities in all parts of Wales." In marked contrast with the mood in the rest of the country, Gwynedd councillors, the local authority where Charles was proclaimed Prince of Wales, voted against another investiture even declaring that the very title should be abolished as it was a symbol of dominance held over Wales by the Royal Family of another country. Proposing the motion, Councillor, Elfed Wyn ap Elwyn, said it was time to "abolish this insulting title" somehow forgetting that far from being another country, we were still a United Kingdom and that Wales received £18 billion in the Autumn 2021 budget from Westminster. The pips would soon squeak if Wales cut itself adrift from such largesse.

As Head of the Commonwealth of 56 independent countries the monarch draws together nations from around the world, a tradition which is generally popular. In 2018 the Prince of Wales was unanimously appointed as Queen Elizabeth's designated successor which was a sign of the continuity the heads of those governments wished to preserve. But life moves on and some nations choose to establish themselves as republics, they hold referendums and dispense with the British monarch as head of state. The royal family does not stand in their way, rather it stresses that loyalty and friendship will endure long after the separation. It is also worth reminding ourselves that Queen Elizabeth supported racial justice and condemned South Africa's apartheid.

There are 195 independent sovereign states in the world, most of which feel the need to have a head of state, and many of them based their protocols on the British pattern because it has been around the longest. Even the Swiss have a president of the Helvetian Confederation which dates back before 1798, although few Swiss would know his name (Ignazio Daniele Giovanni Cassis). The Vatican City is one of the very few sovereign states that does not have a head of state, but then it has the Pope instead.

From time-to-time polls are conducted in Britain to see who still supports the monarchy. For the most part the majority are still in favour – the greatest numbers are among those over 65. Perhaps that is a reflection of how relevant th‹

younger generations view the royal family in their lives, but more likely it is to do with the fact that the older generations see the long-term advantages of stability in this world; nevertheless, the younger generation cheer as loudly as the rest at royal weddings and avidly follow the events of the younger royals on social media platforms.

One line of attack against the monarchy is to suggest it is out of touch and the focus of much of the attack was often against the then Heir Apparent, Prince Charles, in an effort to undermine his popularity and even to break the line of succession by installing Prince William as king – that was something that could never have happened after the debacle of the abdication of Edward VIII in December 1936. It is nothing more than a ploy to weaken the monarchy itself.

Another tactic was to point to the breakup of Charles's marriage to Princess Diana and later marriage to Camilla Parker-Bowles; would the public ever forgive him? As ever, Her Majesty pointed the correct way ahead and gave her blessing to Charles's marriage to Camilla when she declared in her Platinum Jubilee Year in 2022 that it was her "sincere wish" that Camilla be known as Queen Consort on Charles's accession. Camilla has been an example of how to win the public over by quietly getting on with the job of serving the country in her role as Duchess of Cornwall at Charles's side.

She hasn't grandstanded or complained about the initial misgivings, even anger, of the public, she has served her time waiting to be accepted and she has succeeded. On her 75th birthday in 2022 she revealed that she had followed the Duke of Edinburgh's mantra: "Look up and look out, say less, do more – and get on with the job."

Far from being out of touch, Charles was ahead of the game in many ways challenging accepted practices in agriculture, architecture and the environment. He was scorned for admitting that he sometimes talked to his plants, which at least some scientists believe can improve their growth, he backed organic farming in the 1980s, championed the importance of natural preventative healthcare validated by research decades later and warned about global warming in 1990. On architecture, everyone remembers his "monstrous carbuncle" comment about a proposed extension to the National Gallery in 1984, but he later reminded the Royal Institute of British Architects that he was simply referring to inappropriate modern construction juxtaposed to classical buildings. He stressed that he was not against modern architecture but not at the expense of its surroundings, saying that since he was a teenager in the 1960s, he had become aware of "the brutal destruction that was being wrought on so many of our towns and cities." And according to some dairy farmers, he singlehandedly saved their businesses by helping to promote artisan cheesemaking as this BBC item recorded on

26 September 2022:

How King Charles helped save British farmhouse cheese

By Justin Rowlatt
Climate editor

King Charles III is famous for his support of environmental and social causes over the years, but did you know he played a decisive role in the renaissance of traditional artisan cheese in the UK?

It is a perfect example of the way he has used his position to help support the issues he cares about. It may also hint at what a modern Carolean monarchy could look like.

The story begins back in the early 1990s when a series of food scares had shaken confidence in British food. A raft of new hygiene rules designed for industrial cheesemakers was being applied to dairies producing farmhouse cheeses - including a potential ban on the use of unpasteurised milk.

Across the country artisan cheesemakers were teetering on the edge of bankruptcy. Randolph Hodgson was worried, as he had spent the previous decade attempting to revive British cheesemaking by promoting the best produce through his cheese shop in London's Covent Garden, Neal's Yard Dairy.

"I really believed it would be the end of the great tradition of cheesemaking in the UK once and for all," he says.

Mr Hodgson had set up the Specialist Cheesemakers Association (SCA) to lobby for the interests of artisan producers and the association's work had caught the attention of the then Prince of Wales.

Cheese is only as good as the milk that goes into it and the prince was keen to support the high welfare and environmental standards on the dairy farms producing artisan cheese.

He was also interested in preserving traditional British farming and food productions skills. He had become a patron of the SCA in 1993 and got wind of the troubles the industry was facing. His response was typical of his approach to problems, say former advisers. He decided to convene a meeting over lunch at Highgrove, his residence in Gloucestershire.

The King likes "connecting people and organisations in ways that open up possibilities and create solutions", explains his former press secretary Julian Payne.
"King Charles doesn't tell people what to do, but brings them together to see if they can work out a solution among themselves," he added.

Charles invited cheesemakers and cheesemongers to his country pile along with civil servants from the Ministry of Agriculture and government ministers.
Mr Hodgson remembers the 1999 meeting well.

"Do we think it is important to keep these cheeses and traditions going?" Charles asked.

Everyone agreed it was.

"So, what are you going to do about it?" was his next question for the room.

The meeting ended with the civil servants agreeing to work with the cheesemakers to draw up a code of practice to ensure good hygiene in small dairies.
It was, says Mr Hodgson, an "incredibly important moment" in the history of British cheese.

"He wasn't seeking attention for his support, he just brought everyone together and found a path through it all," he remembers.

His intervention worked, says Tim Rowcliffe, a former chairman of the Specialist Cheesemakers Association.

"From that day on, we had a dialogue with authority rather than going to war," he says.

And the industry has thrived.

Up in the hills of west Wales, I met Patrick Holden and his wife Becky who make a cheddar-style cheese called Hafod using unpasteurised milk from their 75 Ayrshire cows.

Patrick says his farm was saved by the efforts of King Charles.

"He saw the need for farmers to add value to their milk," explains Patrick, who says his farm is only viable because he can treble the value of his milk by turning it into artisan cheese.

Patrick is not alone.

There are now more than 700 different British and Irish farmhouse cheeses on the market: "Probably more than the French, dare I say it," laughs Mr Rowcliffe.

Artisan cheese has become a multi-million-pounds-a-year industry supporting hundreds of small farms, thousands of jobs and which now exports British cheese all over the world.

The King has quietly helped drive forward all sorts of other causes by convening meetings, building bridges, and just getting people talking together.
The rules have changed, of course.

Now he is King, Charles must remain politically neutral, but it is unclear if that will prevent him championing the causes he cares about.

such as a state visit, that may mean having to meet unsavoury characters. The Queen hosted countless leaders at state banquets in Buckingham Palace and there can be little doubt that she longed to be as far away from some of her guests as possible. It was reported that she once hid behind a bush to avoid meeting the Romanian President, Nicolae Ceausescu; at least she was usually wearing a pair of gloves when she was obliged to meet and greet. All the other members of the family can do is rush home and wash with hand sanitisers and hope they never again encounter some of the rogues and villains who manipulate their way into their company. It is no use demanding an apology when the army of advisers fails to protect a member of the royal family from an ill-judged meeting because there will be others as it is the very nature of the job to meet, even welcome, heads of state, leading business personalities and figures from the arts on a daily basis. These individuals are being introduced because of what they represent not because of their private predilections which, when they emerge, should not necessarily be interpreted as being endorsed by royalty. What is surprising is that such unfortunate encounters do not happen more often.

It is sometimes questioned why the president of the United States may only serve two terms of office, a maximum of eight years, at the end of which he or she and all their acquired experience in the post are, it seems, no longer needed, and they retire to play golf or occasionally pass comment from the side-lines. They still retain the honorific of Mr President and Secret Service protection, but they are no longer asked, or expected, to contribute to national affairs. By comparison, Queen Elizabeth was able to share her knowledge, experience and wisdom with a succession of prime ministers in times of peace and conflict regardless of which political party may have been in power. The obvious advantages of the line of succession ensure that future kings and queens can benefit from the acquired wisdom of their predecessors by, as it were, the apprenticeship they have served at the feet of their fathers and mothers.

By contrast, continuity is lacking when a political leader is appointed head of state because they will be endeavouring to put their own stamp on the direction in which they want to take their country. This may or may not be in accordance with the direction their predecessor has taken, which in turn may lead to disruption or worse. The monarchy in Great Britain, of course, does not try to influence the politics of the prime minister of the day but, although the weekly conversations between the monarch and the prime minister are held in secret, there is no doubt that any prime minister would have had regard to the advice which they were given by a monarch of such long standing as Queen Elizabeth II, and believed it was worth considering.

The point is politicians are temporary whereas the monarchy in Great Britain is permanent – or at least while the public wish them to remain, as the Queen herself once wryly observed. Even when figures such as Winston Churchill led the country to victory against Germany in World War ll no sooner had peace been declared than he was voted out of office, such is the fickle nature of the electorate in any country. Churchill's eviction from Downing Street after leading the country to great military victory was curiously echoed in 2022 when Prime Minister Boris Johnson was defenestrated by his own MPs despite leading the Conservatives to their overwhelming electoral victory in 2019 with a majority of 80 seats – the biggest Tory victory since 1987.

From a purely commercial point of view, the royal family has value in terms of the amount of tourism it generates. Thousands are drawn to the royal palaces and even the routine ceremonial of changing the guard and Trooping the Colour. However, on special occasions, such as when Prince William married Kate Middleton in 2011, according to the UK's Association of Leading Visitor Attractions the numbers multiplied:

"It saw an additional 600,000 people come to London for the weekend, 60% from UK, 40% from overseas, spending £107m … The

value to 'brand Britain' due to global media coverage was approximately £1 billion."

There is another value members of the royal family bring to the public and that is through their official visits, and for Prince Charles and Princess Anne that meant more than one a day while Her Majesty was getting frailer. Some may dismiss these occasions as merely unveiling a plaque or a whistle-stop tour of a factory or hospital, but they are popular and valuable because they generate interest and support for the causes and charities that they are publicising. How hard can it be, some might say, to unveil a plaque? In itself it is easy, but it might involve long travel, it might require preparation and delivery of a speech and above all it is always done with a smile, a kind word of greeting to a child presenting a posy of flowers. Perhaps not as arduous as working on the factory floor, but a friendly chat with a factory worker and a photograph or fleeting appearance on television is an uplifting experience and one never forgotten. Even the most ardent republican would have gone weak at the knees when meeting the Queen and that was because she commanded respect, and a recognition of many long years of dedicated service to others. Not something many, if any, could ever match.

Occasionally, a royal visit can have a global impact not just for raising money but for a humanitarian cause. The most striking example was the sight of Princess Diana walking through an active Angolan minefield in 1997 to promote the international ban on landmines. A single image of the princess in protective clothing did more for the cause of the HALO Trust than any words or fund-raising campaign could achieve.

Members of the Royal Family are not precluded from everyday jobs, it just depends on how senior they are because that dictates how many royal duties they are expected to perform. When the Queen became too frail to carry out as many official duties as she would have liked other senior members took up the slack. For many those duties become their everyday life. When the Queen succeeded her father, George VI, her husband, Prince Philip, realised that he could no longer hope to continue his naval career and threw himself into his role as her consort, while at the same time energetically supporting charitable causes and creating new ventures, most notably the Duke of Edinburgh's Award Scheme; at his Thanksgiving Service in March 2022 500 charities were represented. When Lord Snowdon was married to Princess Margaret, he pursued a successful career as a photographer, and Princess Anne's children, who do not have royal status, all have independent private lives. In short, just because the extended royal family may be close by birth, they do not represent a drain on the public purse and every charity celebrates royal patronage that it enjoys. It might even be argued that far from owning great wealth, the royal family are merely custodians of their possessions for their successors, unlike the freedom to spend of millionaires around the world, like some bejewelled maharajahs or potentates. .

The reality is if an individual marries into the royal family, their higher profile may mean that they must relinquish otherwise successful careers: Sophie, Countess of Wessex, even after her marriage to Prince Edward, the Queen's youngest son, ran a profitable PR company. But, in due time she closed her agency and came to be an increasingly present figure at Her Majesty's side as she became frailer.

Nevertheless, the cost of the royal family, paid through the Sovereign Grant (sometimes called the Civil List), is regularly used as a stick with which to beat the institution. Republicans point to the 'hidden costs' such as security, which is paid for by the police, and ask the same question every year: Is it value for money? The answer is surely to be found in the unique pulling power of the Royal Brand. When the Royal Yacht HMY Britannia sailed around the world between 1954 and 1997, an invitation to dine aboard was never declined even though each visit was plainly a trade mission, a PR attraction to put it crudely, to draw business communities together and to "sell Britain" and all she had to offer.

The decommissioning of the yacht was regarded by many as a mistake and there is pressure to build a replacement. Britannia was used by the Queen and Prince Philip for their occasional holidays and by Princess Anne and later Prince Charles for their honeymoons, and there can be little doubt that Her Majesty would have preferred to enjoy the yacht in private more often, but the yacht meant work for most of its 44 years and any replacement would fulfil the same role because being a royal is a job. The Firm must deliver every day of the year just like any other business; we, the public, are its demanding shareholders, and every day of the year someone, somewhere, is delivering on our expectations. This is what we take for granted and yet still question its value for money.

In times of austerity, a critical eye is often cast over the sumptuous wealth and surroundings of the royal family, but these go with the job. They are passed along the line as new monarchs are crowned. The money is not somehow squirrelled away into private bank accounts, it is used daily to fulfil the role that they inherit by birth, and the duties they must perform. Working royals cannot have an "off day" when they don't feel up to cutting a ribbon, making a speech or welcoming a visiting head of state – they have to be at their best, every day, which is not something most of us could claim to be. The role costs money, but it is not their money to squander, and a modern, slimmed down monarchy is all too aware of the "optics" of extravagance, knowing full well that their every utterance, their every action, will be scrutinised by those all too ready to criticise. What is the alternative, a cut down, bargain-basement royalty which might resemble nothing more than a well-to-do businessman travelling in business class, carrying his own briefcase accompanied by a PR functionary? Where would be the brand recognition and pulling power? Are we really ready for Buckingham Palace to be turned into an upmarket hotel or for Windsor Castle to become a stately home tourist attraction open to all?

What of all the pomp and pageantry? The gilded carriages, the crowns and the jewels? Are they not all a bit too much of an anachronism in this modern, practical era and should they not all be consigned to museums? Would it not be more cost effective if 'the Firm' really was run like a normal company with modern offices and adequate staff?

But to what end? They would certainly not attract visitors, the mystique and the magic of royal patronage would disappear, some 3,000 worldwide charities would lose their support and the millions of pounds royal attendance attracts. In short it would cheapen the brand if it could still be classified as such. Brands have pulling power; they are instantly recognisable, and the most successful ones endure regardless of whims and fads. As Walter Bagehot, wrote of the monarchy: "Its mystery is its life. We must not let in daylight upon magic."

The glitz and the glamour of state occasions, the ceremonial which can trace its history a thousand years or more make up that mystery and magic; the crowns, the costumes, the uniforms, the marching bands all have an historical link. The colours of the regiments, the tradition and even the very music being played are steeped in customs passed down through the generations. The value of the British Regimental system is that regiments go into a theatre of war as one and come out as one, minus casualties. By comparison, US draftees sent individually to Vietnam, for example, for one year only counted the days to the end of their deployment.

Of course, the celebration of military tradition may be quickly challenged as triumphalism and even warmongering, but it is not, it is a memorial of the sacrifice of generations passed who have enabled the people of the United Kingdom to live in peace, free to say what they want and free to live as they choose.

The traditions surrounding the Royal Family, the very pomp and pageantry which some may dismiss, have a relevance in the modern world because they help us understand and remember what has gone before and without which we would be the poorer today. They represent a rallying point in times of danger and conflict, and they are therefore a unifying talisman to help us triumph in adversity.

No single king or queen needs a building the size of Buckingham Palace, but it is a working office and many of the state apartments are already open to visitors; Charles has suggested that he would need less space and plans, no doubt, were being drawn up to see how the building could be used more efficiently, but it will remain the focal point of the monarchy even though the Queen thought it more practical, given her age and lack of mobility, to spend her final years at Windsor Castle. And that, perhaps, is the point, the royal family may be surrounded by regal splendour and enjoy a privileged lifestyle, but above all they are practical, very much aware of their responsibilities and duties, and as the Duke of Edinburgh would have wanted and demanded at his own funeral and Thanksgiving Service: Keep it simple and let's get on with it.

Our History

"Ingenuity and Genius down the Centuries"

We are witnesses and victims of a concerted attempt, in the republican centred commentary and in academia, to disown or rewrite or diminish our history as though it had never happened in the way that it did. However shrill the hysteria of the campaign against it, we should do neither. We should defend it resolutely, because it is our history and no one else's. We are who we are in part because we were who we were. It is also a useful and enlightening guide to our future. As Winston Churchill observed, 'The further back you can look, the further forward you can see'.

The problem with history in our modern, fast-paced world is that it is regarded as irrelevant, out-moded and, therefore, of little consequence with nothing to teach us. It is not even a popular subject to be studied at university trailing a long way behind computer studies. Worse, we are sometimes even ashamed of our forefathers and would rather everything they stood for – good or bad – was erased. But British history makes us what we are, what attracts people to our shores, our way of life, our attitudes to others, our character. We cannot somehow pretend history didn't happen just because we dislike some of its toughest, even cruellest moments.

The Great Britain of today, in its racial composition, is significantly shaped by the Great Britain of yesterday. Most of our ethnic minorities come from countries, from the Caribbean to Africa to the Far East, where our ancestors arrived uninvited in previous centuries and which they claimed in the name of the Crown. Some of our most successful immigrants were the East African Asians expelled by Idi Amin from Uganda in 1972. Home Secretary, Suella Braverman, said she was proud of her imperial heritage, as her parents had come from Kenya and Mauritius in the 1960s and heaped praise on what they came to know as their 'mother country'. She believed we should celebrate 'the ingenuity and genius of the British people' (*Daily Telegraph* 18 June 2022).

Our biggest critics are those who regard themselves as British but for some reason are at the forefront of campaigns to eradicate the very elements which have combined to make the United Kingdom the country that it is, a land of free speech and free thought. They are the permanently dissatisfied, the people most likely to find fault with life, the envious and the most demanding, and invariably those with the loudest voices. Tradition counts for nothing and is elitist, patriotism is derided, and therefore all traces should be eradicated. Everything, apart from their own attitude, must change. These are the people who want to dig up daffodils because they might be eaten by children, these are the people who want to ban traditions such as tea breaks in cricket matches in case a player has an allergy, and, of course, these are the people who tear down statues of the benefactors of our cities and universities because of their connection to the slave trade, a trade which Britain was at the forefront of banning in 1807 under the Slave Trade Act, not to mention the abolitionist movement that began in Britain in the 18th century, which needless to say is selectively omitted from any argument. The harmless beauty of one attacked by those who refuse to acknowledge that people should take some personal responsibility for their actions, the calm tradition of sharing time with your opponents of the other, and narrow-mindedness of the last are symptomatic of a generation with no regard to tradition, history or perspective.

We cannot pretend that our history did not happen because it contained some dark and shameful episodes. Of these none was darker and more shameful than our part in the slave trade for more than 200 years from the reign of Queen

Elizabeth 1 to the early 19th century. The British did not initiate it. That grim distinction belonged to the Portuguese. But we were involved in this barbaric enterprise more widely and intensively than any other country. Between 1667 and 1807 the British are estimated to have delivered more than three million Africans, from the coasts of Sierra Leone to Angola, into bondage in the Caribbean and North America. Countless thousands more who embarked on the ships did not survive the voyage. Some died of disease or starvation and others were murdered by drowning. The trade enriched the merchant venturers of Bristol and the mill owners of Lancashire. It was one of the engines of a thriving industrial economy.

But the country which profited most from this trafficking in misery was also the country which took the lead in ending it, first with the Slave Trade Act and then with the Slavery Abolition Act of 1833. The second Act was necessary because the institution of slavery survived the first Act. It was a slow and gradual process in the course of which the slave owners were handsomely compensated. But here is the point: we cannot fully understand the achievement of the abolitionists, led by William Wilberforce, unless we also understand the strength of the opposition to them, led by the plantation owners of the Caribbean and the cotton kings of Lancashire, nor indeed by the Africans themselves who enslaved their brothers and handed them over for transportation. The newspaper of the cotton kings was the supposedly liberal *Manchester Guardian.* Our history is woven from a single cloth, and we do it no justice if we try to separate the reputable from the disreputable.

Or to take another example: the reign of Queen Victoria from 1837 to 1901 is seen by many historians (though not all) as an age of progress, reform and prosperity. But in every single one of those years British soldiers were fighting and dying in small wars (and in the Crimea, one big war) to enlarge and defend the dominions of the Empress of India. Her ill-armed 'enemies' ranged from the Zulus of South Africa to the Maoris of New Zealand.

All of this needs to be taken on board by those of us who resist the rewriting of our history in destructive and negative terms. These revisionists are the permanently dissatisfied, the most clamorous naysayers and the ones with the loudest voices. Tradition counts for nothing, patriotism is condemned as elitist, and if these people have their way there is hardly a statue still standing in the country which will be safe from destruction. Sir Francis Drake, pirate and national hero at the time of the Armada, was an early slave trader who also circumnavigated the world (1577-1580) and whose statues may now be vulnerable in Tavistock and Plymouth in Devon. Does it mean everything Drake achieved should be dismissed as not worth recognising. His queen, Elizabeth, wanted to benefit from the trading opportunities in the Americas and Drake saw no harm in attacking Spanish and Portuguese ships returning laden with treasure. It was these attacks which led to the Spanish Armada. Should we be apologising again? What would have been the consequences if the armada had succeeded?

The Scottish philosopher John Locke helped in the drafting of slave-permitting constitutions. Another captain of a slave ship was John Newton who later became a leading abolitionist, and whose hymn *Amazing Grace* was a song of contrition and redemption. *'I once was lost but now am found, was blind but now I see.'* His memorial in Olney, Buckinghamshire, is surely safe.

Statues are history written in stone or bronze, and how can we be true to our history if we pull them down? To be realistic there was probably no way of saving the statue of Edward Colston of Bristol which was thrown into the river by anti-racism protestors in 2020. It was erected in 1895 as a tribute to his philanthropy, but he was a leading merchant venturer and prominent in the Royal Africa Company which not only sold 100,000 Africans into slavery but branded them with its initials RAC. All the traces of his name have been erased from streets and buildings in the city as though he had never lived. The likeliest resting place for the damaged statue, complete with graffiti, will be in a museum. This too is part of our history, and we cannot learn from what we have destroyed.

By a quirk of this history, the Slavery Abolition Act of 1833 still permitted the holding of slaves in two staging posts of the Empire, the islands of Helena and Sri Lanka. These were still under the jurisdiction of the East India Company, through which British power was exercised until 1858.

Britain has always punched above its weight in terms of influence as well as military might. Exploration and the search for new opportunities have always been in our national DNA. We may live on a small island, but we are not little islanders and throughout our history we have explored lands beyond our shores in a spirit of inquiry, of adventure, or trade – and, yes, often of conquest. In 1600 Elizabeth I granted a charter to a trading company which developed into the all-powerful East India Company. It was to be the start of a golden age.

Since we are reviewing the history here, would it really have been better for India if the Company had never existed, and the British had stayed at home? This was a question addressed by Professor Kartar Lalvani, an Indian by birth, in his book *The Making of India – the Untold Story of British Enterprise* (Bloomsbury 2016). And since conquest was enabled by developments in navigation and weaponry, if the British *had* stayed at home, by whom would the Indians rather have been colonised - the

French perhaps, or even the Japanese? Both of them came close. Professor Lalvani wrote:

'Love it or loathe it, the East India Company (EIC) stamped its presence on India, bringing with it triumphs and disasters. For 250 years, from the first intrepid voyages in small ships heading for a land thousands of miles away to its eventual dissolution in 1858, the Company ruthlessly pursued its ambitions. The irony is that such was the strength of the foundations that the much-reviled EIC built in its all-conquering drive, that India in the 21st century is now playing a leading role in enterprises around the world. So, a story about the making of India begins with the EIC: not to examine its motives or morals, but to study the origins of the infrastructure, at all levels, which has enabled India to grow into the nation it is today.'

The Company played a part in extending the Empire and turning the mother country into a maritime super-power. The EIC accounted for half of the world's trade during the mid 1700s-early 1800s before losing its ruthlessly controlled monopoly officially in 1813, but by which time Britain had become the dominant power in the Indian subcontinent following the Battle of Plassey in 1757. But what did it do for

India? On this, Professor Lalvani asked an unfashionable question but one that he was surely entitled to ask as, himself, a child of Partition: was the 200 years of British rule the most progressive two centuries of India's recorded history?

This is the point at which we enter the debate about the merits and demerits of the Empire; and in the present climate of opinion the case for what the British accomplished hardly gets a hearing. But the India of today is bound together by imperial undertakings. The railway construction between 1853 and 1883 saw services operating over 10,882 miles of track, which rose to 37,266 miles by 1922. This of course required the building of bridges on a massive scale and from coast to coast. One of these, across the Soane River near Arrah, was nearly a mile long with space between the double tracks 'for the passage of pedestrians and elephants'. The Curzon Bridge over the Ganges at Allahabad was one of the wonders of the world when it was opened in 1903. Of the earlier bridge at Lucknow the magazine *Engineering* observed in 1870 'Considerable interest attaches to this bridge, inasmuch as when completed it will be the first bridge built across the Ganges, which is prominent alike in the religion and geography of India.'

On the credit side of the balance sheet of Empire in India this surely is undeniable: that without the British in India there would have been little growth in its infrastructure – railways, bridges and telegraphs – and in its democracy. Professor David Heymann of Chatham House, London, said: '...The wide-ranging infrastructure provided by the British helped prepare India for its transformation into a 21st century power.' According to Deloitte, the forecast economic growth in 2024 is strong: 'This will ensure that India reigns as the world's fastest growing economy over the next few years, driving world growth even as several major economies brace themselves for a slowdown or possibly a recession.' (*India Economic Outlook,* July 1922). India is a superpower in the making.

Add to the infrastructure the establishment of the rule of law, a uniform educational system, the adoption of the world's most useful language, the idea of a free press and at least the ideal of a government free of corruption – all these have been transformative in India and elsewhere – though the free press has been somewhat under siege in recent years. In an increasingly interdependent world, our own country has also been enriched; and today generations of highly skilled Indian businessmen and women, scientists and scholars have made their homes in Britain and become leading figures of the community in all spheres of life, and in turn made British society more diverse. The benefits flowed both ways.

On another level the legacy of Empire includes the game of cricket, which is not only played in India but fanatically supported by large crowds. Even cricket is controversial in Anglo-Indian relations. The prominent Congress Party MP (and former UN official) Shashi Tharoor maintains that the Indians actually invented it, although there is no evidence for this and as far as we know it was first played in the Middle Ages by children in the Weald of Kent. We may no longer be the world's leaders in many sports, but along with cricket, we introduced Association Football, rugby football, golf and tennis to many countries. Although even these today can come in for criticism. According to an exhibition at the University of St Andrews, Scotland: "By recreating and imposing British sports in colonised countries, golf and cricket were spread around the world."

So again, what if the British had stayed quietly at home? Would the component countries of our Empire have been better off without us? Were we no more than adventurers, thieves and plunderers? Were we bent only on enriching ourselves at the expense of lesser tribes without the law? In setting out the positives we must not lose sight of the negatives, and in setting out the negatives we must not lose sight of the positives. The campaign being waged against our history lacks these essential qualities of equity and balance.

Yes, there was profiteering, there was slave trading, there was pressure to convert to Christianity, there was pressure to adapt to British culture to the detriment of native traditions. (Not all of which were harmless: in 1829 the British in India criminalised the practice of *suttee*, which obliged a widow to immolate herself on the funeral pyre of her husband.)

The judgement is a fine one, much finer than the professional naysayers would allow; and on the credit side we are now more open and penitent than we used to be about the sins and errors of the past. The slave trade has no defenders and is widely seen as having been a national disgrace, by everyone including the Royal Family which historically benefited from it. (Both Elizabeth I and James II had links to slave trading companies). In a speech in Barbados in March 1922 Prince William, now first in line to the throne, described slavery as 'an appalling atrocity that forever stains our history. It is a source of profound sorrow. It was abhorrent. And it should never have happened.'

Another source of profound sorrow was the Partition of India in 1947, when the British beat a hurried retreat and as more than a million people may have died in the violence that followed. It was an ignominious departure, negligently planned and badly executed. But by the time that it happened the British had succeeded in uniting a patchwork of competing kingdoms on a land mass nearly the size of Europe into one nation (actually two, after Partition) with a recognized government freely elected through the democratic vote. India remains to this day the world's most populous democracy.

None of this is to disparage the extraordinary achievements of the great Indus civilization which flourished 5,000 years before the birth of Christ, but was ultimately unable to defend itself and was destroyed in numerous invasions by barbarians from the north. In this context the British may even be seen as the saviours rather than the plunderers of India. An Afghan warlord, Ahmad Shah Durrani, attacked and ransacked the city of Delhi eight times between 1748 and 1767, at a time when the Mughal dynasty was disintegrating.

However, the Empire was never intended as a charitable enterprise. Throughout it we created a market for British goods and developed exceptional trading links, benefiting economies across the world. We established and maintained global shipping routes and we brought education and literacy for the first time to many nations. English has become the language of science, the language of law, the language of aviation and the language of entertainment. As a result of the industrial revolution in the 19th century, we were able to share technology from New Zealand in the east to Canada in the west. For more than 200 years the British possessions were indeed the Empire on which the sun never set.

The industrial revolution came at a cost. Is it possible that even the gains of mechanisation and invention could also be decried because the living conditions of those crowding into the cities were so appalling that they would have been better off remaining in the countryside? Whenever and wherever there is progress there will be winners and losers. The answer to levelling up society is not to bring down the affluent and successful but to raise up the less well-off through renewed opportunities.

The history of Great Britain is the history of a war-fighting people. Our victories are well remembered in battles long ago that we won, and long forgotten in those that we lost. Our regiments, warships and warplanes brought us out on the winning side in both the world wars of the 20th century – in partnership in both with our allies, principally one of our former dominions, the United States of America. Our wars thus far in the 21st century, in Iraq and Afghanistan, have been notably less successful, and we have lessons to learn from them. But victory in World War II won for us a global standing which remains. We are founding members both of NATO and of the United Nations. We are permanent members of the UN Security Council alongside China, France, Russia and the

United States. We are the smallest of the five, but we have a voice equal to theirs, having been granted that status according to Oppenheim's International Law in 1945 'based on their importance in the aftermath of World War II'. The world has changed radically since then, but the structure of the United Nations has not. (And it is surely to our credit that we were the only one of the permanent members not involved in any way in the wars in Indo-China from 1946 to 1975.)

The British armed forces fulfil a number of roles. One is the defence of the realm and the deterrence of hostile powers. Another is to take part in the peacekeeping operations of the United Nations (in which their high quality makes them most welcome contributors). A third is ceremonial. The Army has shrunk in size from 400,000 in 1960, when conscription ended, to less than a quarter of that today. Some of its regiments have vanished completely and some have amalgamated with each other two or three times over. But it is notable that the Guards regiments (Scots, Irish, Welsh, Grenadier and Coldstream) *and their bands* have survived relatively unscathed. This is because of the contribution they make to Great Britain PLC in drawing so many visitors to these shores. They are also linked to the institution of monarchy, being both the monarch's personal bodyguards and (like all British soldiers) owing their allegiance not to the government of the day but to the monarch.

Our Queen Elizabeth served longer than any of her predecessors. Only ten per cent of her subjects have known any other monarch. The republicans' slogan is 'Elizabeth the last'. We can be sure that with her passing the nabobs of negativity will have a field day. No institution will be exempt and no historical figure. William Shakespeare is renowned as the world's greatest playwright of the 16th and 17th centuries when he composed his plays and poems which have been translated into almost every language; but that is not good enough for the naysayers, who criticise his work as racist, anti-feminist and homophobic and even urge its removal from school curricula.

This too will pass. Our history tells us that as a nation we are prone to spasms of sabotage and self-harm. One of these was the dissolution of the monasteries in the 16th century. Another was the abolition of the monarchy in the 17th century. The monasteries were not restored but the monarchy was. Now again the saboteurs are at the gates. In due course their revisionism will fail, and we shall send them packing. If our history teaches us anything it is that extremism will be tolerated only so long before the natural order of things is restored.

Our Democracy

"Freedom of Choice, Freedom of Speech"

The point of our democracy is it allows us the freedom of choice, however, that is interpreted as the right to protest about everything we dislike without regard to other opinions. Worse, other people are increasingly being aggressively prevented from having an alternative point of view in case it might cause offence. Books, films, TV programmes today all must walk a narrow path of politically correct plots for fear of a backlash from the critically ill-informed. Life is unfair and complicated, people are complicated, and people are diverse, but that doesn't mean that every aspect of complexity must be included in every story line for fear that one minority or another might feel excluded, which stretches the credulity of the reader and viewer.

Our democracy has a fail-safe mechanism built-in, and it is called an election. If we don't like the politics of one party, we can vote for change at the ballot box every five years without recourse to violence or rioting. Sadly, even that mechanism which is open to all is at times not good enough and protests follow if the vote doesn't go our way. When the country voted by a narrow majority to leave the European Union in the Brexit vote it provoked widespread protests and a constant bickering from politicians and commentators bent on undermining the validity of the result or even overturning it. Even some civil servants hold a "remain bias" according to the then attorney general, Suella Braverman, who she claimed were blocking government efforts to cut EU legislation. She said they were unable "to conceive of the possibility of life outside the EU." (*Evening Standard*, 3 July 2022). Every setback is laid at the Brexit door and never a word is uttered in acknowledgement of its benefits; there are arguments on both sides, but they can have no impact on the final outcome of the vote, so let's move on.

Britain is an unwritten constitutional monarchy with the monarch as the head of state with executive power exercised by the government led by a prime minister. This division was established in 1689 with the Bill of Rights which states that the monarch cannot rule without the consent of Parliament. Our constitution is a system which has evolved over the centuries.

Jack Straw, Secretary of State for Justice in 2008, said: "The constitution of the United Kingdom exists in hearts and minds and habits as much as it does in law." It has been built on Acts of Parliament and legal precedence rather than a formal written constitution such as that of the United States.

The Westminster system with two houses of parliament has been copied in all or part by many other countries; the Liberal statesman, John Bright, said on the 18 January 1865 that "England is the mother of all Parliaments." If it is so good, why are so many determined to destroy the arrangement? As we have seen some regarded the monarch as head of state as an anachronism and yet both the Queen and our democracy was and is admired the world over. The answer is that some regard it as elitist which is anathema for those who would prefer a socialist even communist model. Others just object to the status quo and would prefer to dismantle the whole democratic edifice, others still who come to this country, happily enjoy the freedom and the benefits, before complaining that they are bring oppressed or worse turning to terrorist acts ostensibly in retribution for ills committed by governments, past and present, in other parts of the world.

It is no use explaining to them the benefits of an impartial monarch who can caution and advise, it is pointless arguing that no communist state has succeeded in bringing prosperity and lasting happiness to its people, (Vladimir Putin brooks no criticism under pain of 15 years imprisonment let alone the terror he inflicts on his neighbours), and nothing can convince a radicalised terrorist that murdering innocent civilians in an act of revenge is pointless savagery.

The people of Britain have enjoyed their rights since 1215 when the barons forced King John to sign the Magna Carta at Runnymede giving every citizen the right to be tried by their peers and protection from unlawful arrest.

Protection from unlawful arrest that is a joke, some will cry, fearing stop and search rules. But why were these rules introduced, because crimes were being committed, drug taking and selling, carrying guns, knives and machetes. Who needs a machete to go about their lawful business on the streets of Britain? It is for our protection some will say, but protection from whom – others carrying knives, other gangs? If you deal in drugs, drive without a licence or insurance, break into someone's house, or steal a car you can be expected to be stopped. It is not prejudice or unfair, it is the law. Once again it comes down to taking personal responsibility and that does not include the right to break the law.

The democracy of the United Kingdom gives us protection from those who would like to diminish our strength. When we voted in 1973 to join the European Economic Community

(Common Market) it was regarded as a mutually beneficial trading bloc. But the Common Market evolved into the European Union which sought to impose laws and restrictions centrally on all its members and there was an inevitable conflict of interest. Whose laws took precedence – national or European – and was it right that EU laws were being enacted by unelected bureaucrats as they were perceived?

For the majority of Britons, it became too much and, of course, we left in 2020 following a democratic vote, much against the wishes of David Cameron, the Conservative prime minister who had called the vote. But he accepted the result and felt in the circumstances that the honourable thing to do was resign.

Sometimes events occur over which governments have no control. When the former Prime Minister, Harold Macmillan, was asked what the greatest challenge for a statesman was, he replied: "Events, dear boy, events." And so it proved to be in 2019 with the outbreak of the Coronavirus pandemic. Every country in the world attempted to deal with it as best they could; illness and loss of life was tragic, and the economic impact of businesses closing and people losing their jobs was colossal. In the UK the job retention furlough scheme was introduced which, as of November 2021, cost the UK £70 billion. This happened at a time when all nations were trying to tackle the impact of climate change and ambitious pledges were being made at UN Climate Change Conference (COP26) in Glasgow to reduce carbon emissions.

But inflationary effects were beginning to bite, energy costs started to rise, the cost of living was driving families to food banks and then in 2022 Russia launched its invasion of Ukraine pushing fuel costs still higher, leading to food shortages and the terrible consequences for the Ukrainians themselves.

In the midst of these pressures in the UK there were protests by "eco-warriors" demanding the government went further to achieve Net-Zero targets unconvinced by the promises made at COP26. Energy companies were targeted, their offices attacked, windows broken, and paint daubed on walls. At the end of their protesting day, no doubt the protestors jumped on a bus or tube train, returned home, switched on their lights and boiled their kettles for a cup of tea never questioning for a moment where the power to do so came from. The same warriors drove onto motorways and glued themselves to the road denying others their right to go about their lawful business saying it was the only way to make the government pay attention, before either being arrested using up police resources or, of course, driving themselves home in their petrol- or diesel-powered cars. Their rights trumped others' freedom of movement.

Peaceful protest is one of the perks of our democracy, but the peaceful element has been abandoned. Is it really their right to hurl abuse and rocks at the police who are trying to restore order and then complain about the police being heavy handed? And yet it was acceptable in protestors' eyes to injure police officers in clashes with anti-establishment protestors in Parliament Square on Bonfire Night, 2021, it was acceptable when a policeman on duty to marshal football fans in Manchester in May 2021 suffered life changing eye injuries, and it was acceptable for police to be bombarded with beer cans thrown by anti-lockdown protestors in London in December 2021.

No-one is above the law and even when Prime Minister, Boris Johnson, was fined £50 for spending nine minutes at an impromptu birthday party for him in No10 Downing Street, he apologised, said he didn't believe his attendance was a breach and paid the fine. His opponents gleefully seized on the moment and called for an inquiry as to whether or not he had deliberately misled parliament and demanded his immediate resignation along with that of his chancellor, Rishi Sunak, who had also been fined £50. In the end it was, of course, academic as both men resigned, leaving only the Parliamentary Privileges Committee to see how they could force Johnson to quit as an MP as well.

There is a peculiarly British relationship between the executive, the judiciary and the church which dates back hundreds of years and which from time to time has resulted in conflict. Historically the most infamous occasion was Henry VIII's desire to divorce his wife, Catherine of Aragon, and the refusal by Pope Clementine VII to grant an annulment. It led to the English Reformation and the break of the Church of England from Rome in a series of Acts of Parliament passed between 1532 and 1534, most notably the Act of Supremacy declaring that Henry was Supreme Head on Earth of the Church of England.

The principle is that each has its own sphere of influence and authority, but today that sphere is being transgressed because everyone has an opinion and cannot resist voicing it. When the Archbishop of Canterbury, Justin Welby, chose to say that the deportation of illegal immigrants from Britain to Rwanda (a member of the Commonwealth) was "ungodly" in his Easter sermon in 2022, he was criticised by Prime Minister Johnson. Archbishop Welby, while acknowledging that the details of the decision were a matter for politicians, said: "...the principle must stand the judgement of God and it cannot." The prime minister told Conservative backbenchers that the Rwanda deal was a good policy and it had been "misconstrued" by the archbishop. He refused calls to apologise saying he was more concerned about stopping the illegal activities of the people traffickers which were costing lives.

It is hardly the stuff of Henry II and Thomas Becket and the king's plea for someone to "rid me of this turbulent priest" in 1170, but it is surely for the church to preach on spiritual matters in general and avoid the political policies of the government in particular.

But today nothing is off limits, and everyone has an opinion which is the privilege of living in a free country, however, that means that those opinions once offered in public are fair game to be criticised in their turn. If church leaders choose to enter the political fray, then they must be ready to accept the fightback. In this instance, Boris Johnson refused demands from the opposition to apologise for what Sir Keir Starmer, the Labour leader, called slander, but he did express his surprise that the archbishop had chosen to focus his Easter sermon on Rwanda rather than the Easter message. He might have added: Render unto Caesar the things that are Caesar's, and to God the things that are God's.

In 2019, Johnson's government crossed swords with the judiciary in the midst of the Brexit crisis. The prime minister had advised the Queen that parliament should be prorogued for five weeks exploiting royal prerogative powers. The courts were divided: the English courts refused to intervene in the political process, while the Scottish appeal court believed they could. In the event the Supreme Court ruled that the government's prorogation was unlawful "because it had the effect of frustrating or preventing the ability of parliament to carry out its constitutional functions without reasonable justification" stating: "This court has … concluded that the prime minister's advice to Her Majesty [to suspend parliament] was unlawful, void and of no effect. This means that the order in council to which it led was also unlawful, void and of no effect should be quashed."

It was an unusual event, which was acknowledged by Lady Hale, president of the Supreme Court, when she said: "The question arises in circumstances which have never arisen before and are highly unlikely to arise again."

The principle in Britain is that parliament enacts the laws and is superior to the executive and judicial branches of government. Once a bill has been enacted by parliament and becomes law it is then for the courts to interpret. The difficulty today is everyone insists that their human rights are being broken at every turn.

The Human Rights Act 1998, which was to be replaced by the UK's own British Bill of Rights before the idea was shelved, is there to ensure everyone is treated with fairness, dignity and respect. The government's aim was to restore what they call "a proper balance between the rights of individuals, personal responsibility and the wider public interest". The later suggestion was that the (Truss) government was prepared to leave the European Convention on Human Rights (ECHR) and introduce tougher rules to prevent illegal migrants and foreign criminals trying to rely on the Convention to avoid being thrown out of the country.

There are 16 rights in the Human Rights Act ranging from the right to life and freedom from slavery and torture to the right to marry and education. But while slavery in many guises continues to this day, two rights in particular are being ignored or abused: the right to freedom of expression and the right to freedom of thought, belief and religion.

The right to freedom of expression is the right being most obviously ignored. Just because we disagree with another person is no reason to refuse anyone the right to speak. Such was the extent of 'silencing" at some universities that the Higher Education (Freedom Of Speech) Bill was laid before parliament to "strengthen the legal duties on higher education providers in England to protect freedom of speech on campuses up and down the country, for students, academics and visiting speakers."

Presenting the bill, the then Education Secretary, Gavin Williamson, said: "It is a basic human right to be able to express ourselves freely and take part in rigorous debate. Our legal system allows us to articulate views which others may disagree with as long as they don't meet the threshold of hate speech or inciting violence. This must be defended, nowhere more so than within our world-renowned universities."

In 2021, the lecturer, Kathleen Stock, faced banners and flares at Sussex University demanding that she be sacked for expressing her views about transgender ideology with stickers on her building about the "transphobic s*** that comes out of Kathleen Stock's mouth." In October 2021 she resigned from her post after 18 years' teaching.

Attitudes towards Brexit on campuses are never far from the surface and, according to a YouGov poll, of 820 academics questioned one in seven noticed a hostile climate towards their political beliefs. The attitude has become that it is wiser to conceal one's views and conform rather than risk hostile protest. Hardly the stuff of rigorous academic research.

Hate speech is anathema to freedom of speech; it can incite or simply justify violence and today it is fuelled by the easy access to social media. As ever freedom comes with responsibility; it is one thing to say you disagree with Islam, Christianity or Judaism, but it is quite another if what you say encourages other to resort to violence or to discriminate against a particular group because of their ethnicity, disability or sexual orientation.

On the other hand, one is perfectly at liberty to stand up against a policy such as abortion because of one's religious beliefs, but standing up does not mean being free to daub red paint on clinic doorways or intimidate clients seeking the services of those clinics. Nor for that matter does it mean forcing one's opinion about any rights – gay, transgender, LGBTQIA+, etc., - on everyone else. By all means believe what you will but keep it to yourself unless asked, don't feel it is necessary to march every year in protest lest others decide it is appropriate to demonstrate in support of their own beliefs with which you may disagree. It is the British way to be tolerant and modest, much like being asked how you are. The inquirer is not usually that interested in your long list of ailments. The safest answer is: No complaints!

Sometimes it can be subtle, sometimes the hatred can be blatant such as when the Islamist preacher, Anjem Choudary, was convicted on terrorism charges in 2016. On his release from prison two years later his supporters gathered round him on the street waving banners claiming oppression of Islam with one stating that the United Nations, USA, UK and Syria were all criminals, and another that Islam was the solution. They had that right thanks to our benign democracy where people can make such claims, unlike Putin's Russia where criticism can cost you your freedom. Equally others can disagree just as vigorously, and they should be allowed to do it throughout the UK without fear of violent retribution.

Since the 1800s people have gathered on a Sunday at Speakers' Corner in London's Hyde Park to make public speeches and engage in rowdy debate with all-comers. Karl Marx, Vladimir Lenin and George Orwell have all stood on a soap box to argue their point of view.

Sadly, while we live in a United Kingdom where all laws apply equally, it is also a racially divided kingdom as well as being racially diverse, and that is because people naturally congregate with their own kind, all of which is perfectly acceptable. We are undoubtedly a multi-cultured society and there is nothing wrong with celebrating one's own culture. What is not acceptable is when, as a result of social behaviour, whole districts become no-go areas for anyone from a different ethnicity, and where even the police tread warily. We are not an integrated society. A 2011 census in Bradford, for example, showed a declining white population there in the previous ten years (78.27% falling to 67.44%), but also a falling Indian population (2.67% down to 2.59%) compared with a rising Pakistani population (20.41% up from 14.54%). Bradford is increasingly a Pakistani city.

Such division can lead to violence sparked by a relatively mundane event. The Notting Dale Riots in London on 29 August 1958 are said to have been triggered by an assault on a Swedish woman by her Jamaican husband. A group of white people tried to intervene and later that night white youths went on the rampage attacking the homes of West Indian residents. The rioting continued until 5 September. Wiser heads have prevailed in recent years and today the Notting Hill Carnival is a celebration of parades, dance and music, attended by some two million people.

Neither the initial alleged assault nor the subsequent riots can be condoned, but the problem arises because instead of integrating fully, ethnic groups, no matter what their socio-economic group might be, choose to live alone. Even the mink-lined ghettoes of the very wealthy do nothing to preserve a healthy, cohesive society.

As noted earlier, immigrants are attracted to our shores for a multitude of reasons and the numbers are forecast to keep rising. According to the think tank, British Future, the number of non-EU workers, students and family relatives granted visas had already increased by more than 50% to more than 840,000 since the UK voted to leave the EU. The director of British Future, Sunder Katwala, said: "Immigration this year (2022) could be higher than any other year in recent British history.

This has come about through active policy decisions by the government to make immigration easier." (*Daily Telegraph*, 26 April 2022). Indeed, Home Office data showed that nearly a million (994,951) foreign nationals, including workers, family relatives and students, came to live in Britain in 2021. And the government announced plans to make it more attractive for the brightest and best international graduates to be granted long term visas to work in the country.

No-one is turned away from the UK so long as they enter legally. The country has benefitted from all-comers by absorbing the best of their talents and even adopting some of their cultures and traditions. That is our natural way of life, and it is preserved and protected by our democracy. If anyone dislikes that freedom, freedom of speech and of belief, then they should live elsewhere and not attempt to coerce others with their mistaken ideologies. Stand on a soap box at Speakers' Corner and make your case, but don't be offended by the barracking and don't complain that you are being discriminated against because it is an absolute certainty that someone will disagree with whatever you are saying because that is their democratic right.

Our Judiciary

"One Law for All"

Just like our democracy, our judiciary has evolved over the centuries and continues to evolve, although some may argue that it is time to bring back the stocks to shame criminals in public, although the ducking stool for witches may be going too far! Today it is having to change in the face of political correctness and people's human rights regardless of how heinous the crime. "Prisoners" became "residents" or "clients", and "cells" became "rooms". But the then Justice Secretary, Domini Rabb, decided in 2022 that such woke-ism should change because it undermined the public's confidence that criminals were being punished for their offences.

Perhaps surprisingly, the judiciary was only formally recognised in law as being an independent branch of government with the passing of the Constitutional Reform Act of 2006 making it an express statutory duty of the Lord

Chancellor and ministers of the crown to protect the independence of the judiciary.

Today there are three divisions of the British judiciary system: the King's Bench, The Chancery Division and the Family Division with appeals processes above those. It was not always that way. In Anglo Saxon times there was trial by ordeal which might involve grasping red hot stones to see how quickly one healed or, as mentioned, the ducking stool; if you survived you must be a witch, if you drowned you were probably innocent but then it was too late.

The king was heavily involved and appointed the first judges who knew where their loyalties should lie, but gradually over time judges would follow laws passed by parliament which replaced local laws making the legal system common to all – Common Law. Today 95 per cent of criminal cases are dealt with by the most junior branch in the magistrates' courts and only the most serious offences reach the Crown Court. In Scotland there is a three-tier system: the High Court of the Judiciary, the sheriff courts and the justice of the peace courts. The Supreme Court of the United Kingdom operates across all British jurisdictions.

As a result of the size of the British Empire many countries have a legal system based on the British model which is adversarial as opposed to inquisitorial like the Juges d'Instruction of France. In an adversarial situation prosecution and defence make their case before a judge and jury. The jury, which is drawn from members of the general public, decides guilty or not guilty with the judge taking a neutral position advising on points of law and passing sentence. In an inquisitorial situation it is the judge who leads much of the questioning of witnesses.

Various nations can trace their legal system back to the days of the British Empire. The foundations of Canadian law are based on English law, when it was still a colony, and also French civil law. The written Canadian Constitution today is the supreme law, and the courts can override laws passed by the government if they are found to contradict the constitution. Under the terms of their Constitution Act 1982 all legislative ties with Britain ended.

In Kenya, before its independence in 1963, the legal system was entirely based on the English legal system with its roots in the East African Order in Council 1897. It gradually evolved to allow for one court for Europeans and another for Africans with local tribunals to settle disputes overseen by village elders. Today, like England, there is a Supreme Court, Court of Appeal and High Court operating under the Constitution at two levels: Superior and Subordinate Courts.

Hong Kong still retains a Supreme Court with British judges, but in March 2022 the president, Lord Robert Reed, and colleague, Lord Patrick Hodge, resigned from the Hong Kong Court of Final Appeal citing the threat to civil freedoms from Beijing.

In England and Wales, the threat to the judicial process for some can come from a different direction. There are 3 million Muslims in the UK and many turn not to the British courts for justice but to their own Sharia courts which come under the UK's Tribunal Court system but have no legal status or legally binding authority under civil law. Not every Muslim necessarily approves of this, but many have little choice in towns and cities with large Muslim populations. It is not uncommon to see banners proclaiming: "You are entering a Sharia controlled zones – Islamic rules enforced." Sharia law, loosely translated as Islamic law and which encompasses religious observances, demands that women, for example, should wear the Hijab whether they want to or not.

This is Britain where we have the freedom of choice and of speech, but for millions that choice has been removed by men sitting in judgement as self-appointed judge and jury, and so often women are treated as second class citizens. An independent review in 2018 into the application of Sharia law in England and Wales found that Sharia councils themselves acknowledged that there was discriminatory practice against women. White girls are certainly disregarded completely as evidenced by the rape and sexual exploitation of 1,400 girls by Muslim men in Rotherham between 1997 and 2013; it continued for so long because authorities were fearful of being called racist.

We are not the multicultural society we may wish to be. The former prime minister, David Cameron, said "multiculturalism had been a failure" adding: "We have even tolerated these segregated communities behaving in ways that run completely counter to our values. This hands-off tolerance has only served to reinforce the sense that not enough is shared… What we see – and what we see in so many European countries – is a process of radicalization."

The Social Mobility Commission found in 2017 that only 6% of the Muslim population were in professional jobs blaming Islamophobia and racism. But where does the blame lie when the choice of so many Muslims is to live apart, following their own rules, dressing in their own way as though they are living in a different country and many even refusing to learn the language? When the earliest influx of immigrants began arriving in the UK in the 1950s and 1960s, it was fondly imagined that their future generations would be assimilated, settle down and learn the English language. But that never happened. There are many exceptions most notably in the Indian community who have gone on to be high achievers. But if you refuse to mix with the rest of the population, if you only watch satellite broadcasts in your own language, then you will always be apart. One can't talk about segregation if it amounts to wilful segregation, an almost aggressive determination to be apart from the majority of the community. Why should it be necessary for every legal document to be printed in a multitude of different languages? In the Middle East you either speak Arabic or English if you want to conduct business or even communicate. It should surely be a legal requirement for all immigrants to the UK to learn English as a second language and not to insist on interpreters or for every leaflet to be printed in their own language. It is impossible to live and experience all the benefits of the country and its culture if you cannot understand what is being said or written.

The tendency to live in close-knit, even segregated, communities is not limited to Muslims. Jews, particularly ultra-Orthodox Jews tend to live apart. They also follow strict rules on behaviour, how they interact between men and women, and how they dress and what they eat.

A report published by the Institute for Jewish Policy Research found that ultra-Orthodox Jews would make up the majority of British Jews before the end of the century fuelled by the birth rate of seven children per woman compared with the overall UK birth rate of 1.93. Their determination to stand apart and look different is manifested by many Hasidic men wear suits and black hats in the style of Polish nobility of the 18th century and typically have hair curls called "Payos" hanging down in front of their ears. It is certainly distinctive and sends a clear message to the rest of the community that they want to keep apart,

Jews also have their own judiciary in what is called the Beth Din which covers civil arbitration and religious rulings but has no jurisdiction over criminal or family law. The oldest Beth Din is the Court of the Chief rabbi in London which was established in the early 18th century.

In February 2022, anti-Jewish hate incidents reached a record high in the UK according to the Community Security Trust charity and notably the highest volume of university-related hate ever recorded. Our freedom of speech and belief is under threat even if violence is sparked by events far away in the Middle East. Regardless of religious differences, violence can never be condoned and should be condemned by all faith leaders who believe they sit in judgement over their followers. There is one law to keep order in the UK and no preacher, regardless of their right to free speech, can defend any breach of the peace.

But all is not right in the British judicial process, most notably the backlog of cases awaiting trial. According to the Law Society, before the Coronavirus pandemic there was already a backlog of some 40,000 cases waiting to be heard in the Crown Courts. This ballooned with the onset of the Covid virus. Many senior law practitioners pointed to difficulties in recruitment particularly for the low pay in criminal legal aid work, restrictions on the number of sitting days and trials being adjourned at short notice; some barristers resorted to strike action.

Despite these problems the UK is a largely peaceful country although police records show a sharp increase in violent crime and sex offences in recent years. Nevertheless, there is support even for those accused through the legal aid system. And everyone has the right to have their case heard by members of a jury at the Crown Court even if their case starts at the Magistrates Court in England and Wales or Justice of the Peace Courts in Scotland.

In short, the British judicial system is regarded as one of the best in the world which is why people seek to be tried here rather than in any other country if their case permits. Of course, there are miscarriages of justice which are a tragedy both for the wrongly accused, who may have been jailed for many years before being acquitted on appeal, and for the families of the victims, who are searching for justice. None of which makes the system fatally flawed or the juries wilfully corrupt on reaching the wrong verdict; the alternative of summary judgement by a judge sitting and sentencing alone is too dangerous to contemplate. Perhaps the most senior law practitioners could be more diverse, perhaps they should be paid more to attract more applicants and no doubt the whole judicial system needs more government funding, nevertheless we should applaud what we have got for fear of something worse.

Our Military

"Essential Preparedness"

Fearing something worse is surely the *raison d'être* of the British military capability. No British government intends to set out to attack another country if unprovoked, despite what Vladimir Putin may have suggested in his own defence for attacking Ukraine in 2022. Indeed, the invasion by Russian forces of that country highlights how necessary military capability remains, and is likely to remain for years, if not generations, to come.

As if to underline the point, on taking up his appointment as head of the British Army in 2022, Gen Sir Patrick Sanders, warned all ranks and civil servants in an internal message that the Russian invasion of Ukraine demonstrated the need "to protect the UK and be ready to fight and win wars on land." He went further saying the army and his allies must now be "capable of … defeating Russia." (*BBC*, 20 June 2022)

Ukraine has taught us many valuable lessons. It has taught us that what used to be called conventional warfare is still with us despite the proliferation of high-tech weaponry. Tanks and long-range artillery were used in the fight for Ukraine. If men and machines can still be thrown at an enemy when the so-called Unblinking Eye of armed drones and air-breathing, hypersonic missiles capable of flying at 3,800 miles an hour are available, it at least shows us that we must be prepared to counter what might be called a crude, traditional threat, a type of warfare unseen in Europe since World War II. While no British personnel were actually on the ground in Ukraine, thousands were sent to countries bordering Russia and Ukraine, and millions of pounds were committed in the shape of military hardware, intelligence gathering, training and, one assumes, additional covert activities behind the scenes.

In 2022, the European Union signalled that Ukraine would be welcomed as a member and given candidate status along with Moldova. The EU Commissioner, Ursula von der Leyen, said: "We have one clear message – and that is, yes, Ukraine deserves European perspective, yes, Ukraine should be welcomed as a candidate country. This is on the understanding that good work has been done – but important work remains to be done. Entire process is merit based, so it goes by the book and progress depends entirely on Ukraine. So, it is Ukraine that has it in its hands." (*BBC,* 17 June 2022).

Was all this warmongering, should we have stood back and watched while Russia invaded its neighbour, raping and pillaging as it went, or was it right to lend our support to the military and civilians of Ukraine who wanted nothing more than to live in peace? No one would doubt that the defeat of Hitler's Nazi Germany was a victory for all right-thinking people, but would pacifists have wanted the world to sit by and watch what happened in Mariupol?

In a speech at the National Army Museum the UK Defence Secretary, Ben Wallace, said: "Putin, his inner circle and generals are now mirroring the fascism and tyranny of 70 years ago, repeating the errors of the last centuries' totalitarian regimes." He was speaking as Vladimir Putin told the huge annual Victory Day parade in Moscow's Red Square on 9 May that what he called a "Special Military Operation" had been necessary because of provocations by the West. (*BBC*, 9 May 2022). A perhaps cynical view might suggest that Putin called it a "Special Military Operation" because if he had called it "war" he would have had to pay the widows and families of men killed in the fighting much bigger financial settlements.

If the United Kingdom is so defensive in its military posture, one might ask is it really necessary to have a Navy, Army and Air Force with garrisons in position around the globe from the Falkland Islands to Kenya, Qatar, Singapore and the United States as well as being one of the five recognised nuclear powers? The answer is, of course, yes, precisely because it is called upon in a wide range of capabilities, not only peacekeeping and defensive, but also in humanitarian situations, such as when assisting countries affected by famine, floods, earthquakes, or other natural disasters. A particular British curiosity is the fact that Britain has never liked standing armies which is why the Navy, Army and Air Force have to be voted for anew every year by Parliament, perhaps to remind them who is in control.

Some may be surprised at the range and number of threats facing the world today including the United Kingdom. The government's own list shows the threat capability that every nation faces:

The Threat

- State-based threats
- Electromagnetic railguns
- Space
- Hyper-sonics
- Cyber
- Global security post COVID-19
- Novel Weapons
- Climate Change affecting regional instability

- High Energy weapons

- Bio-security threats

- Violent extremist groups

- Sub-threshold

- Capability overmatch in certain areas

- Weakened global institutions

- Over exposure through globalisation

- Deniable proxies

- Chemical, biological, radioactive and nuclear

- Commercially available drones.

(www.gov.uk)

The list demonstrates that the United Kingdom, and other countries, face challenges on multiple fronts including those that the military describe as being below the threshold of armed conflict. In times of humanitarian catastrophe, we always turn to the military to help us resolve the problem, and then all too quickly we question why so much money is being spent on defence. A pacifist or conscientious objector is hardly likely to turn away from the military hand reaching out to pluck them from a flood.

But consider for a moment where the battlefields of today really are. They're not just on the traditional open plains where tanks may confront other tanks, they may be single chemical attacks in an underground station with sarin gas as we saw in Japan on 20 March 1995 which killed 14 people, or in the city of Salisbury in the UK on 4 March 2018, when Sergei Skripal, a former Russian military officer and double agent for the British intelligence agencies, and his daughter, Yulia Skripal, were poisoned by a Novichok nerve agent. Any terrorist group today with sufficient funds can obtain a sophisticated drone armed with lethal weapons, let alone the capability of a national government.

In a stark reminder of what might be at stake, Jen Easterby, director of the US Cybersecurity and Infrastructure Security Agency, warned: "Should the UK face an attack on the scale previously inflicted on Ukraine's critical national infrastructure sites, businesses and the public should not expect to receive advance warning.

"Preparedness is therefore essential. And our defences must be in place, ready for whatever comes," she said. (*Daily Telegraph*, 12 May 2022)

Britain is ranked as the eighth most powerful military force according to Global Firepower, compared with Russia at second behind the United States. Russia has 70 million people available for military service made up of volunteers and conscripts. By contrast UK Armed Forces personnel stood at

148,000 in 2021 most of whom are full time. However, size, as the world saw in Ukraine, does not count for everything, professionalism and even the willingness to fight count for much more. As one Ukrainian soldier put it, they were fighting for their freedom, while the Russians were fighting for money. The Ukrainians' ability to resist the Russian onslaught and drive them back has impressed military observers; Mr Wallace said even the British forces could learn lessons from the Ukrainian fighters.

Another lesson the UK has learned from the Ukrainian war was just how real the threats to UK and European security were. The Conservative government committed to spending £42.4 billion in the defence budget in 2020/21, or just over 2% of GDP, making it the third largest global defence spender. Labour opposition said it should be more. If the Treasury can find more money, the mood in the general public seemed to be in favour of supporting the defence initiative, which was a remarkable difference from the protest at Greenham Common in Berkshire in the early 1980s against the presence of nuclear weapons being sited at the RAF camp. The last cruise missiles left in 1991 but the camp remained in place until 2000. The peace camp was not entirely welcome particularly by some in the local community who argued that the protestors did not appreciate the defence issues at stake.

The Campaign for Nuclear Disarmament, founded in 1957, gained renewed support in the 1980s; in Scotland the protests centred on the Trident missile base near Glasgow, while in England and Wales they were against the deployment of Cruise Missiles. Its membership dwindled over the years but increased when the former prime minister, Tony Blair, made a commitment to the development of nuclear energy in Britain.

Unilateral nuclear disarmament is an idealistic proposition and one never likely to be contemplated. The theory being that no-one is ever going to press the red button and if no-one actually had the capability the world would be a safer place. No doubt, but of the nuclear-weapon states – the USA, Russia, China, India, Pakistan, the United Kingdom and France – none is likely to give them up. Israel may have nuclear weapons but won't admit to it, North Korea is boasting that it almost has the capability, and Iran is moving closer. Accidents can happen. Speaking at the Centre for strategic and International Studies in Washington, Sir Stephen Ludgrove, the UK's national security adviser, warned of a "dangerous new age of proliferation" and the risk of miscalculating our way into nuclear war because the world did not have the same safeguards of Cold War negotiations to improve relationships. (*Daily Telegraph*, 28 July 2022).

Putin threatened the world that he was thinking the unthinkable as his forces became stalled in Ukraine by saying in March 2022 that he had put his nuclear arsenal on "special combat duty regime" having warned the West that what he perceived as its interference in the war would trigger consequences "never before experienced in your history." (*Financial Times*, 7 March 2022). Although he seemed to soften his tone when he said there could be "no winners" in a nuclear war in an address to the Tenth Non-Proliferation Treaty (NPT) Review Conference at the United Nations. He claimed that Moscow had "consistently" remained faithful to the "letter and the spirit" of the NPT. (*Daily Telegraph,* 2 August 2022).

If there are individuals even contemplating nuclear strikes, there will always be a requirement for countermeasures and a strong credible defence capability. World peace is wishful thinking as history tells us.

A cursory glance at the Internet, lists some 40 wars or conflicts continuing today somewhere in the world predominantly in the Middle East, Africa and Mexico. One of the most protracted is in Afghanistan where no outside aggressor has prospered for long. The British were forced out in 1842 as they tried to build a defence against the Tsarist Russian designs on India. The Soviet Union in turn invaded on Christmas Eve 1979 and eventually left humiliated ten years later in 1989 driven out by the Mujahideen ably supported by the CIA. But the weaponry left behind helped the Taliban drive out US forces in 2021 bringing an end to America's longest running war. Although Washington kept its guard up and did not hesitate to kill the Al Qaeda leader, Ayman al-Zawahiri, who had been given sanctuary in Kabul despite Taliban assurances to the contrary, on 1 August 2022. President Biden said "justice has been delivered" when he authorised a precision drone attack with Hellfire missiles killing al-Zawahiri as he stood on the terrace of his luxury home.

The wretched country has been left in the grip of hard-line zealots where education for girls is banned and full-face coverings for women in public have been imposed. The worry is that Afghanistan and other countries become a breeding ground for terrorists who are prepared to stop at nothing to make their point. The military must be smarter which means more investment into smarter weapons on land, in the air and at sea. But any extra money needs to be well spent. Air Marshal Edward Stringer, former director-general of Joint Force Development, wrote: "We might well need to spend more on defence because the world is not safe and stable. But before we waste money reinforcing yesterday's ways of fighting, let us first assess from where the real future threat emanates…let us work out how to buy what we need not what the Services want, to put resource is behind that theory of winning, and in a less profligate manner than has become the norm." (*Daily Telegraph*, 15 July 2022)

Putin's Victory Day parade on 9 May 2022 while typically vast revealed a diminishing power with many 'out-dated' weapons on display. But that is no reason for Britain not to invest £10 billion in four Dreadnought submarines as part of its new nuclear deterrent, for example, in addition to their ability to remain undetected. The operative word being deterrent. If a leader like Putin chooses to show off their own thermonuclear devices or North Korea provocatively test fires inter-continental ballistic missiles, then the world must be prepared to dissuade them from even contemplating using them in anger.

A new Cold War may already be upon us, so, far from disarming, a nation such as ours must be ready and equipped with the very latest ordnance. When Putin deployed his most technologically advanced T-90M tank in Ukraine he must at least have been worried that it was so easily destroyed by a Javelin anti-tank missile. His only alternative appeared to be long range artillery bombardment as he successfully and brutally used in Syria and Chechnya. But even those tactics appeared to be on the wane as we moved into the autumn of 2022 as he ran low of both ammunition and troops.

The flow of weapons around the world is on the increase not diminishing. The United States is the biggest exporter and Saudi Arabia is its biggest client – 22% of US exports. According to Amnesty International the flow of arms to the Middle East grew by 87% between 2009-2013 and the trade in general is at its highest level since the end of the Cold War. This doesn't make the world a safer place, but it does reflect the world's concern about the increased threat from many directions.

Britain is the second biggest arms dealer in the world according to the UK Defence & Security Exports organisation, selling everything from bombs to fighter jets; our 'customers' include France, Germany, South Africa, the United Arab Emirates and Saudi Arabia; 60% of UK defence exports go to the Middle East.

The question, therefore, is can we afford to take our military for granted or should we increase investment in them well beyond the NATO members' commitment of 2% of national GDP?

It is plain that the world is a dangerous place, and the threats are multifarious, so like the boy scout we must be prepared for every eventuality. We need professionally trained troops who need to be experts in their field, not necessarily large in number. We need to equip them with the very latest technology for protection, not necessarily attack. And we need to be ever vigilant about the threats which may come from within and be 'home-grown' as well as coming from overseas. Some argue that an army of some 80,000 is insufficient given the commitments the UK is making. On 11 May 2022 Boris Johnson visited Sweden and Finland and pledged to support both countries were they to be attacked. The two countries, which are historically neutral, both immediately said that they intended to apply to join NATO which Putin had expressly argued would be a sign of the West's aggression towards his country and achieving precisely what he wanted to avoid. (Their application was initially vetoed by Turkey who later dropped their opposition.) But committing British forces ever more widely might be spreading our resources too thinly. If we want to help other nations defend themselves then we must support our military. In the late summer 2022, six months after the start of the war, Europe was reported to be wavering in its commitment to supporting Ukraine as economic pressures at home began to bite; where should their priorities lie – protecting Ukrainians from Russia or bolstering their own finances and energy supplies with dire warnings of electricity blackouts?

Perhaps surprisingly, Britain still has laws drawn up to protect the country from German spies in World War 1. Now new laws (the National Security Bill) were to be enacted to adapt to changing circumstances. Ken McCallum, MI5's director general, said: "State actors are stealing not only national security secrets, but our cutting-edge science, research and technology. They are attempting to interfere covertly with our democracy, economy and society. We see coercion and, at the extreme, direct threats to life." (*Daily Telegraph,* 11 May 2022)

Our freedom of speech carries with it a heavy duty of responsibility. There is no freedom to incite violence, there is no freedom to spread hatred and there is no freedom to travel to this country if your intention is to disrupt law and order. Our police, armed forces and our intelligence community must all be equipped and ready to protect that freedom. If we are to face a new prolonged Cold War, we must be willing to act without fear.

Apart from British support for Ukraine in the face of the Russian invasion, the country is still involved in security operations in Iraq and Syria as well as protecting and intercepting vessels on the high seas. In the intelligence field, MI5 reports "…over 10,000 disguised approaches from foreign spies to regular people up and down the UK, seeking to manipulate them." (Security Service MI5, 14 July 2021).

It is Britain's openness and freedom that we all should cherish which at the same time makes us vulnerable to attack, but it is also our determination to defend the weak and the vulnerable which makes us ready to fight their corner as best as we can. The former does not make us weak, and the latter does not make us aggressive, but we must be realistic. If the rest of the world in so many places is a threat to our values, then we must defend those values forcefully. And if our friends and allies are equally threatened, then it must be right to offer them the same defence where legally possible. A bully must always be confronted.

Can killing ever be justified because that is what military action amounts to? If we are not prepared to support our armed forces, then who will protect us when it is plain that the threat to our way of life and even our lives are at stake? War today can be precision guided by using a remote-controlled drone which may be operated from a completely different country, or it can be indiscriminate artillery fire. The result, it can be argued, is the same – death. We may never know how many died in the Ukraine war as bodies were buried in mass graves and the Russians even resorted to cremating their own dead in the field. Either way it is a brutal business, but one which cannot be simply wished away. While there is a threat, whether that be from a neighbouring power or, indeed, an ideology which seeks to convert the world to their own way of thinking and believing, then we will need a shield of protection.

The Stockholm International Peace Institute (SIPRI) reported (25 April 2022) that global military expenditure reached an all-time high in $2.1 trillion in 2021 despite the economic collapse due to the Covid-19 pandemic. The world is not ready to step back, and Britain will be ready to help as it demonstrated by the AUKUS trilateral security agreement between the UK, Australia and the USA in the face of what SIPRI observed: "China's growing assertiveness in and around the South and the East China seas have become a major driver of military spending in countries such as Australia and Japan."

Neither Australia nor Japan wants war with China, but everything depends on Beijing's attitude to what it considers to be its own territory, much like Russia and Ukraine. America made its point clear when the US House of Representatives Speaker, Nancy Pelosi, flew to Taiwan on 2 August 2022 – the most senior US official to visit for 25 years. Immediately, China's Foreign Minister, Wang Yi, said "Those who play with fire will not come to a good end, and those who offend China will be punished." (*BBC*, 3 August 2022). A four-day naval and air blockade of the island followed as China conducted live fire exercises.

In the end the argument comes back to value for money. Do we in the UK really need more ships and submarines? Do we need more aircraft carriers and fighter jets? Do we need all those people in military uniforms? Should the whole defence budget simply be redirected to building more houses, cutting our energy bills or supporting the health service?

The answer surely is that we have no choice. Far from being safe from attack, we are under assault from multiple directions (see Threats above) and if we simply mothball the military and all our defence capabilities, we will not be able to conjure up an army when a threat becomes too great to ignore. We are under attack overtly and covertly, and the threat is already critical. We are under constant cyber-attack, we are under attack from terrorists and religious fanatics seeking to impose their own rules, Europe is under military onslaught and the very real danger is that Putin, or others like him, will not stop in Ukraine. If a peace accord is ever to be reached in such circumstances, it is always from a position of strength, even though the West's attitude towards Putin was hardening as the fighting continued – by August 2022 the US had pumped $12 billion into the conflict - and the mood was shifting towards complete isolation of the Kremlin rather than seeking a peace accord. Hitler did not stop because we asked him to, he stopped because he was roundly defeated.

The only real debate is about numbers. Can we rely on fewer solders if we have superior technology producing the same or greater firepower? Do we have enough fighter jets or again will drones render manned planes redundant – why risk an expensively trained pilot when the drone can hover for hours waiting for the right moment to fire its rocket? In Ukraine where Russia could not establish superior air cover, the generals simply ordered their long-range artillery to destroy everything regardless of military or civilian value.

Like every government department, the military must be cost effective and efficient. Fewer personnel with the most sophisticate equipment can deliver effectively anywhere in the world against a less well-trained but greater force using out-dated weaponry. The object of the exercise is to prevent a war starting in the first place. If you launch a rocket, we will blast it out of the skies before it reaches its target like Israel's Iron Dome – an all-weather defence system. If you try and send in a column of tanks, our Unblinking Eye in the sky drone will track it, and even the individual commanders, and destroy them. The message is clear – don't attack in the first place.

However, regardless of our preparedness, there will always be someone ready to try. The tragedy of the 9/11 attacks in New York only took a few determined individuals, albeit backed by others who planned the assault. It wasn't a great army, but America with its sophisticated military machine was taken by surprise. Our intelligence community and our military must think the unthinkable on our behalf. We cannot afford to take them for granted because our lives depend on them. We cannot just assume they will always be there without making some commitment to maintaining their strength and fighting capability. It costs money and from time to time it costs the lives of the young men and women who are prepared to risk all just to keep us safe.

Our Police

"Running Towards Danger"

Bobbies on the beat. That maybe how we would like to think of our police force. Somehow ignored much like a soldier until something goes wrong, we are mugged, or our car is stolen. Then we want them right away. The crime must be thoroughly investigated, and the culprit locked up for good.

Although the image of Sir Robert Peel's trusted crime fighters – the 'peelers' – armed solely with a wooden truncheon may today be a quaint historical memory, his foremost principle remains: Police are the Public, Public are the Police. All officers know that they police by consent of the British people, unlike many countries they do not instil fear among the average law-abiding citizen. But it is a contract between public and police which is fragile. On his appointment as the new Metropolitan Police Commissioner in July 2022, Sir Mark Rowley said: "Our mission is to lead the renewal of policing by consent which has been so heavily dented in recent years as trust and confidence have fallen."

In the same month a report into the sexual abuse of 1,000 children by predominantly Asian men in the Telford area between 1989 and 2021 concluded that the police and key authorities had turned a blind eye to the offences for fear of being accused of racism or dismissing complaints as child prostitution. (*Sky News,* 12 July 2022) While critical of police and local authorities primary blame must rest with the men who perpetrated the crimes and somehow thought it was acceptable behaviour to groom and sexually abuse the children. Those in authority rightly apologised for their failures but most of the real offenders escaped justice leaving their victims to suffer in silence.

Nearly six million crimes were recorded in England and Wales in the year ending December 2021 and theft was the most common offence, according to the Crime Survey of England and Wales. It sounds a big number, and each individual theft is a personal violation as far as the victim is concerned, nevertheless it is relatively low, and the United Kingdom is 174th in the international list of the most homicide cases.

What has changed in recent years is the spike in violent crimes and sex offences. To cope with the changing pattern in crime and increased terrorist threat a significant number of the British police, once renowned for being unarmed, now carry guns. The exception is Northern Ireland where all police carry side arms, and their patrol cars are armoured.

According to Home Office figures 6,853 officers out of a total force of 123,171 were armed in 2021 – the most visible are around the Palace of Westminster and standing at the gates to Downing Street. But the actual use of their firearms is rare. Thames Valley Police have only opened fire on a suspect once in their history. (*Underzone – Police Specialists – Firearms Officers*).

How has the trust in police to which Sir Mark Rowley referred been so dented? According to polls by YouGov the trust varies widely. In London, following the murder of Sara Everard by an off-duty policeman on 3 March 2021, trust in the Metropolitan Police fell sharply with only 33% saying they were confident in them dealing with crime in their area, while outside London 65% said they trusted their local forces. And in January 2023, the conviction of David Carrick, a serving Metropolitan police officer, for the rape and sexual offences against 12 women over a 21-year period had left trust in policing "hanging by a thread", according to senior police officers. (*BBC* 19 January 2023).

The feeling is that police are unable to investigate every minor offence so why bother reporting it; crimes in England

and Wales where someone was charged hit a new low in the year to March 2019 which saw the rate falling to just 7.8%. The former Metropolitan Commissioner Cressida Dick acknowledged that too many cases were going unresolved explaining that sorting vast amounts of phone and computer data was partly responsible. (*BBC*, 18 July 2019).

The government announced in 2021 a recruitment drive to find an additional 20,000 police officers with every force declaring that they need more to meet increasing demands. We are all familiar with the TV images of police raids to break up drug dens or dramatic footage of police chases, but it is the mundane drunk and disorderly crowds outside pubs and clubs on a Friday night, the abuse from foul-mouthed members of the public, which are the usual fare for the average police officer. These are the same men and women those same drunks will call upon if they are the victims of petty crime or physical abuse.

Recruitment is a challenge because not everyone is prepared to stand up to a criminal or even just a drunk. There were 12,000 fewer officers in 2021 than there were in 2010 and recruitment from all sectors of society is a problem. The police force in England and Wales is predominantly white (92.7% in March 2020) with Asian, Black, Mixed and Other ethnic background making up 7.3%. When she was Home Secretary,

Theresa May, criticised Britain's forces for not employing more black, Asian and minority ethnic officers.

Respect for, even fear of, the police has disappeared in some parts of society, most notably among the Black Caribbean community, and they are very much taken for granted until, of course, they are required. There are bad apples in the force as in every walk of life, mistakes are made including wrongful prosecutions, but the pressure is on them as crime rises and offences become more complex. A Home Affairs Select Committee inquiry also reported in 2021 that: "Evidence to our inquiry shows that there is a significant problem with confidence in the police within black communities. We were very concerned to see that confidence in the police among black people has fallen in recent years and the gap in confidence in policing between White and Asian people on the one hand, and Black and Mixed ethnicity people on the other hand, has grown." (*www.parliament.uk*)

Policing has had to change to cope with increasing levels of violence, but there is a desire to get police out of their patrol cars and to be seen pounding the streets as they once did as a deterrence against "low level offending and anti-social behaviour." West Midlands Police, for example, reported that the proportion of thefts resulting in a charge had halved from 9.9% in the year ending March 2016 to 5.6% in the year to June

2021. (*Daily Telegraph*, 29 December 2021). Increased visibility of the police is a return to the original concept of patrolling the streets to deter criminal activity in the first place. This is what the average law-abiding citizen takes comfort in. Before the establishment of the Metropolitan Police in 1839, a magistrate called Henry Fielding appointed a small force dubbed the Bow Street Runners in 1749 because he saw members of the public were trying to enforce the law themselves. Today, we have something similar with the Neighbourhood Watch Scheme with people being alert and reporting anything suspicious to the police. Everyone has the power to make a citizen's arrest, however, they are warned about taking unnecessary risks. But sometimes instinct takes over.

Steven Gallant, a convicted murderer on day release in London, tackled Usman Khan who had stabbed two people and was threatening to blow up a suicide vest, with a narwhal tusk on London Bridge in 2019. Eventually police arrived and shot Khan whose vest turned out to be a fake. Gallant received a rare pardon from the Queen for his courage.

While much of the above paints a sorry picture, the police of the United Kingdom compare favourably with the rest of the world. Generally, they do not carry guns which is the same as only 18 other countries and reflects well on our crime rate. Nevertheless, crime is the greatest source of deadly violence across the globe according to the United Nations Office on Drugs and Crime: "Criminal activity is responsible for many more deaths worldwide than armed conflict and terrorism combined." (*UNODC, Global Study on Homicide 2019 (Vienna, 2019).*) Perhaps that is because armed criminals fear no painful retribution for their crimes. If they are caught and convicted, they face a few years in prison only to be released back on to the streets after time served with "good behaviour". Capital punishment for murder was suspended in the UK in 1968 and for treason in 1998 when it was completely abolished.

Our police have a thankless task, on the one hand having to marshal demonstrations, domestic disputes, neighbourly quarrels and drunken brawls, and on the other they have to risk their lives in car chases, or the threat of a lone terrorist bent on making a name for themselves in a bid for elusive martyrdom. They are always the first to be called in the face of danger, and more often than not, they tackle the situation unarmed just by talking quietly and patiently. At the end of what is a long shift when they may have had to face any of the above, they return home before it is time to meet the challenges all over again. When we complain about a long commute or a delayed train journey, when we moan about the service we have received from a client, it is comforting to remember that in the course of our work we haven't been challenged at the point of a gun. These are the men and women who run towards the danger the rest of us flee in panic. They are the men and women who stand shoulder to shoulder pushing back often hostile crowds and protestors who think nothing of dropping concrete blocks on them as they struggle to restore order. (18-year-old jailed for dropping a five stone concrete block onto a policeman in Bristol – *Daily Mail*, 12 December 2011.) In a survey of 10,987 serving police officers and staff by Police Care UK in 2016, 81% said they had experienced at least one physical injury or mental health issue due to their police work.

The future style of policing will change to reflect our society. If more people resort to violence, the police will match that with equal force. They will look intimidating in their protective vests if more people choose to carry knives, they will be armed only to match the threat they face and they will only draw their weapons and open fire as a last resort not as a first reaction. The UK is not the Wild West, even the most dangerous armed criminal is given a loud verbal warning to give themselves up, even that there might be a police dog on hand. There is no shoot first and ask questions later policy. The onus is always on the criminal to give themselves up or not to turn to crime in the first place.

Our NHS

"Time to look in the mirror"

Let's get the criticism out of the way. The NHS is top heavy, creaking under pressure from all sides, serious, even catastrophic, mistakes are made, and it is expensive. According to recent (2020/2021) figures the government spent £192 billion on health and care services in the UK. A study by the think tank, Civitas, estimated that dealing with our health was costing the country annually about £10,000 per household. (*Daily Telegraph,* 23 July 2022). It clearly needs an overhaul which doesn't simply mean more money. As we, the taxpayers, give our hard-earned money to the government every year, it could be argued that the NHS is not really free. However, we can turn up at any accident and emergency hospital and casually expect to be treated as often as we like, day or night, and we do not have to pay a penny. We are so casual about it that we assume it will always be there, somehow just waiting patiently for us to demand its attention. Indeed, anyone who has just arrived in this country who happens to fall and break a leg or sprain an ankle or even has a stroke or heart attack will be treated with the same professional care as someone who has lived in the country all their lives. No-one will ask if they can afford to pay for the surgery or where they come from before even considering their emergency, great or small.

So, yes, the NHS, founded in 1948 when Aneurin Bevan was Minister of Health, is free at the point of delivery. That year every household in the country was sent a leaflet which stated that the NHS would provide: "…all medical, dental and nursing care. Everyone – rich or poor, man, woman or child – can use it or any part of it. There are no charges." The whole point of the NHS said the leaflet was to relieve people of money worries in times of illness.

And, of course, we still complain.

Some ten million operations are performed in England alone every year and everyone on a waiting list wishes there could be more. If you are in severe pain in need of a hip replacement no honest reason provides any comfort if your operation is pushed back by other more urgent emergencies. In 2022, more than 6 million were waiting for pre-planned operations and of these more than 23,000 had been waiting for more than two years, although that number was declining as patients agreed to be treated further away from home where there was spare capacity, with travel and accommodation costs paid for by the NHS.

The problem, of course, was exacerbated by the Covid-19 pandemic, which pushed hospital resources to the limit, and as the virus subsided all those cancelled operations suddenly swelled the backlog.

If anyone has been taken to hospital by ambulance and been left sitting in a queue of other ambulances outside waiting for admission, it is not the ambulance crew's fault, nor the hospital's, nor the nurses', nor the doctors', it is because of capacity.

Your waiting may have started earlier, as anyone who has called for an ambulance will testify. Non-emergency cases may have to wait hours before a paramedic arrives at the door with an apology but with unfailing good humour. It was not their fault.

For all the long delays, for the occasional disaster, even incidents of malpractice, for which there is never any comfort, there are countless millions of success stories which go unremarked in the news. These are not the astonishing feats of recovery after prolonged treatment, but the mundane care which overworked medical professionals carry out every day, bandaging that ankle or plastering a leg.

Overworked and some might say under-paid, it isn't always the answer but so often it comes down to money and how those billions are spent. The biggest charge laid against the powers that be is that the NHS is top heavy with bureaucracy and those at the top are being paid too much; the focus is on form filling not primary care. The think tank, Policy Exchange, found that the number of officials working in the Department of Health and NHS England had more than doubled in the two years since the start of the pandemic while nursing staff had increased by 7%. (*Daily Telegraph*, 16 May 2022.) There is no doubt that senior management are handsomely rewarded but the argument there is that to attract the brightest and best in any field requires generous compensation. The question which needs to be asked is do we need quite so many managers? Equally, to attract junior nurses, who are on the front-line working long hours, should command just rewards. A large part of what is required is careful analysis of value for money to ensure that the extra funding always goes to the front-line. Hospitals used to be run efficiently and ferociously by indomitable matrons whose word was law.

No-one claims that everything about the NHS is perfect but while the service is changing and attracting recruits from different backgrounds and ethnicity – 42% of medical staff working in the NHS are from black and minority ethnic background, nurses from overseas make up half of all recruits, and 34% of doctors joining the health service in 2021 were from abroad according to NHS Digital – there must be sensible debate about thinking the unthinkable of working with the private sector to relieve the burden, and even to consider alternative ways of providing for our own healthcare through compulsory health savings or insurance as happens in other countries.

To what extent is the private sector already involved in our National Health Service? To quite a large extent is perhaps the surprising answer and in reality, a vital cog in supporting the health service. According to the Department of Health and Social Care £9.2 billion was paid to private health providers who were able to take on additional NHS cases. Beds are available, the treatment is available, the question is how to make the combination work more effectively.

But when we have stopped complaining about how the NHS in all its guises is failing us, is it time we looked in the mirror at our own shortcomings – another significant part of the problem?

According to the King's Fund, in 2019 64% of adults in England were overweight, 28% were obese and 3% morbidly obese. Other statistics show that as a nation, the UK ranks 33rd in the depressing obesity charts at 27.8% which still equates to about 35 million overweight people. A later study by Cancer Research UK found that obese people will outnumber those with a healthy weight within five years – that's 42 million overweight people by 2040. (*Daily Telegraph,* 19 May 2022). Diabetes UK underlined the problem when it reported in April 2023 that 64% of adults in England were overweight or obese. In a telling rebuke for the younger generation, Lt Sergeant Farren Morgan, a fitness instructor in the Coldstream Guards, condemned TV advertisements suggesting it was alright to be fat and happy in yourself. He said young army recruits should be happy, but they should also be healthy. He said: "I think [as a country] we're scared to see what's going on [with obesity] and deal with it." (*Daily Telegraph,* 26 July 2022). Not everyone can be as fit as a Coldstream Guardsman, but a step in that direction would not go amiss.

Not all diabetes is caused by overeating but its impact on the NHS is substantial. The Diabetes Medicine journal predicted that the service's annual spending on diabetes would reach £16.9 billion by 2035. NHS England states: "Around 9 out of 10 people with diabetes have Type 2 diabetes and there is strong evidence that its onset can be prevented or delayed in those at high risk, through improved quality of diet, through increase in physical activity, and through successful weight loss." The message is crystal clear: cut down on the chips and the chocolates and the beer, resist the buy-one-get-one-free offers and start taking some exercise. One in six people occupying hospital beds now have diabetes and according to research many of them needn't have been there in the first place. There are 200,000 new cases of Type 2 diabetes in England every year.

Sam Patel, director of Day Lewis Pharmacy one of the UK largest pharmacy chains, hammered home the point when he said easy access to free NHS care was making people "lazy about taking care of their own health. (*Daily Telegraph* 4 April 2023).

You can get lung cancer even if you have never smoked a cigarette in your life, but it is the most common form of the disease – obesity being the second biggest cause of cancer – and it is estimated that 90% of all cases are caused by cigarette smoking. (*Reuters.com* 16 June 2010).

Not only can smoking kill, but it can also leave people with debilitating illnesses such as emphysema. A 2021 report by Landman Economics commissioned by ASH – Action on Smoking and Health – found that more than 1.5 million people in England alone require social care as a result of smoking and that it costs the NHS an estimated £2.5 billion. (*Ash.org*, March 2021). No-one has to smoke, and still less, no-one should have to endure second-hand smoking which over time can be just as damaging to one's health. Yet again it comes down to personal responsibility; should a child have to suffer because the parents refuse to quit? The chocolate, the tobacco and the alcohol industries are there to make money, we just must learn to say no more, occasionally. That won't make the ambulance service any more efficient, one might argue, but if you don't have to call one in the first place it will free them up for a real emergency. In October 2021, NHS 999 staff answered a record 1,012,143 calls.

How does the NHS compare with the rest of the world? A recent study commissioned by the BBC[3] suggests that it is a world leader in terms of free access to treatment, but it lags other countries in terms of available beds, numbers of doctors and nurses, CT and MRI scanners, and funding. Only 20% of people questioned felt the NHS was adequately funded but the majority (97%) felt the responsibility for staying healthy lay with the individual.

The competing pressures are underfunding and staff shortages against a determination that free access continues. England alone was short of 12,000 hospital doctors and more

---

[3] Dayan M, Ward D, Gardner T, Kelly E, 'NHS at 70: How good is the NHS?' Health Foundation; 2018
(https://www.health.org.uk/publications/nhs-at-70-how-good-is-the-nhs)

than 50,000 nurses and midwives, according to a report in 2022 by the House of Commons Health and Social Care Select Committee. Everything has been complicated by Covid 19 which has created the serious backlog in treatment across the board and ever-longer queues for operations, for ambulances or even just to see one's GP; it is forecast that there will be a shortage of 8,900 full time GPs by 2030/31 (www.health.org.uk). It's a vicious circle, if we can't see our GP for what might be considered a relatively minor ailment, we know we can simply wait in line at Accident and Emergency, and so the queues get longer.

We used to be more resilient dealing with cuts and bruises ourselves but because we know our local hospital is just round the corner and will deal with the problem for free that is where we go. "Research has shown that between 15 and 20% of people who turn up at A&E should more appropriately have gone to their GP," according to Doctor Chris Moulton, consultant in emergency medicine at the Royal Bolton hospital and vice president of the Royal College of Emergency Medicine. (*Mail Online*, 9 April 2018) The problem there is GP practices are also overstretched and one can wait days for an appointment which may only amount to a short telephone consultation in which more serious complications are missed. A fallback position is to ask our local pharmacy for advice and help, but higher costs and staff shortages are forcing many to close with the NHS reporting in 2022 that the number of community pharmacies in England was at its lowest (11,636) in six years.

One of the most pressing problems is the ageing population. There are already 12 million people aged 65 and over, according to Age UK, and of those some 500,000 are over 90. With old age comes frailty, illness and the inability to look after oneself. That is not necessarily a problem with an extended family to care for you, but the burden shifts to the health service otherwise. There is increasing concern about so-called "bed-blockers" where patients come into hospital, are treated but cannot return to the community because there is no-one able or willing to provide round the clock care for them; according to government figures there are 105,000 vacancies in the social care sector. None of which is the fault of the NHS.

In 2000, the World Health Organisation considered that France provided the "best overall health care" in the world which is admirable, but the refugees and economic migrants travelling from conflict zones do not stay in France as they make their way through Europe, they head for the UK where they know that healthcare for all its faults is free and where there are so many other benefits. The threat of possible deportation of asylum seekers to Rwanda had little impact on the numbers attempting to cross the Channel. In fact, the government anticipated the numbers doubling in 2022 to 65,000, many no doubt trying to capture the opportunity before the Rwanda threat came into force, legal challenges notwithstanding. The estimated net increase in immigration overall to the UK in the year to June 2022 was 504,000 – a figure which was worryingly high for some as fears grew about the increasing strain on the existing housing shortage and public infrastructure, NHS capacity and social services capability.

We Britons may take the NHS for granted but every immigrant and visitor see it as providing a comforting safety net amid all their other challenges. It is bad enough having to find shelter and work in a new country, but knowing that if you fall ill, as we all do from time to time, there will always be a helping and caring hand to pick you up, is at the very least reassuring.

There will be thousands, if not millions, of patients of every age from tiny babies to centenarians who are in varying degrees of pain who need urgent and immediate care, and for those individuals it is an emergency. But at the end of a very long waiting list there will be treatment, free at the point of delivery. For countless billions of others around the world there is no queue because there will never be any treatment and for that at least we must count our blessings. It goes without saying that matters could be improved: more nurses, more domestic medical training instead of relying on international recruits, certainly less bureaucracy and more of the money saved being redirected to the hard-pressed front-line, all of which would improve life expectancy. But imagine for a moment that the NHS did not exist, if prescriptions for the elderly were not free, if an ambulance could not be summoned by phone 24 hours a day manned by highly trained paramedics however long the wait, then consider just how fortunate we are.

No-one could have predicted the Covid-19 pandemic which brought the NHS to its knees but did not overwhelm it thanks to exceptional, herculean efforts by doctors and nurses and other supporting healthcare staff. But it has caused major problems of delayed treatment and life changing surgery which given time will be overcome. What everyone wants as a starting point is to be able to ring up their GP to get a face-to-face consultation within a week or two so they can assess without delay how serious one's symptoms are without recourse to attending A&E. It will happen, it will take time and it will take targeted funding, which in turn will improve treatment and recovery rates across the board. None of which will lessen the immediate pain one might be in, but it would be infinitely worse without the NHS as it is. We treat it in the same casual manner we might summon a taxi, so convenient, seemingly waiting in the rank for our call. Just occasionally the rank is empty, the drivers busy elsewhere, then we may have to wait a little longer, it may even be raining to add to our discomfort until, finally, a taxi appears round the corner, and that is when we realise how fortunate we are and how in our complacency we just assumed that when it was our turn the service would always be at our disposal.

Our Freedom of Belief

"A Right to Disbelieve"

Great Britain is fundamentally a Christian nation, many still attend church services and many still believe in God. The King is head of the Church of England, which is known as the established church. On the other hand, for many, particularly the younger generation, the only religious events in their lives are weddings, baptisms and funerals. There is too much going on, it seems, for them to stop and reflect, religion has been side-lined, it certainly is not cool, but woe-betide anyone who threatens to disrupt our long-held traditions with their outside influences and corrupted interpretation of classical faiths.

According to research by the Tearfund organisation: "Christianity is still the predominant faith in the UK with over half (53%) or 26.2 million adults claiming to be Christian, while other faiths account for 6%. So, three out of five people in the population are affiliated with faith and the remainder claim to have no religion (39%)." (www.tearfund.org) Although, the Office for National Statistics 2021 Census of the population of England and Wales suggested that only 46.2% of the population consider themselves to be Christian. (*BBC*, 29 November 2022)

Unusually for a national parliament, representatives of the church are entitled to take their seats in the House of Lords, to join in debates and vote on legislative matters. They include the Archbishops of Canterbury and York as well as 24 other bishops, collectively known as the Lords Spiritual, as opposed to the Lords Temporal, the secular members of the Upper House.

In the House of Commons, the nearest one gets to religious input is the Chaplain to the Speaker – the first one being appointed in 1660. The parliamentary day starts with poorly attended morning prayers with members (and peers in the Upper House) traditionally facing the wall behind them which stems from the difficulty of kneeling while wearing a sword. (www.parliament.uk).

None of this paints a picture of a particularly religious country; we seem to take it or leave it, only having second thoughts, perhaps, at the end of our days. Although not everyone has those, as the French writer and philosopher,

Voltaire, (and others) is supposed to have said on his deathbed when asked if he would renounce the devil: "This is no time to be making enemies." However, when appropriate at times of solemn remembrance we bow our heads and make our own silent prayers and we do this alongside others of different faiths and no faith.

The nation has developed from paganism which was still practised when Julius Caesar's armies arrived in 55-54BC, through the arrival of the Anglo-Saxon and Viking invaders with their worship of gods such as Odin and Thunor, to the dispatching of a monk called Augustine by Pope Gregory 1 to the court of King Aethelbert in Kent where he was well received, and, through his influence, Christianity eventually spread throughout the land.

Great Britain is a tolerant nation when it comes to other religions, but it will always draw the line when there is any suggestion of outspoken proselytising which can sound threatening to both other individuals and to the nation's core beliefs, however tenuously held.

Somehow it is very un-British to hold extreme views on anything, with the possible exception of football clubs or cruelty to animals, so the image of a man (it is always a man) standing in front of a group of 'worshippers' directly attacking the customs and behaviour of the people in a country where he has been accepted, is intolerable. The firebrand style of address, designed to whip up outright hostility towards their hosts and fellow citizens, is unwelcome and, worse, can lead to violence. It is our absolute right to be a so called: 'unbeliever' or 'infidel', we will respect your customs when we are in foreign lands, but when you are here, you should respect ours.

We are tolerant about the style of dress, we are tolerant about the right to follow any faith or none, but we will always be intolerant about anyone claiming to hold all the answers and to be the only true faith, particularly if ill-informed followers are convinced that they have to take up arms against the innocent to convince them otherwise or in some misconceived notion that they are doing their god's will, in the certainty that paradise awaits them should they die in the process. The concept of a vengeful god welcoming suicide bomb attacks against non-believers or even casual passers-by is too fanciful to contemplate. The simple fact of life is that no-one knows what the future holds for us, if anything, at the end of our days.

Extremism is an ugly feature of so much today. Religion is a dominant issue of the 21st century and together with cultural barriers it is keeping communities apart. But the UK always strives for consensus to enable us to navigate these complexities without causing offence and with the ultimate aim of drawing us closer to one another to share wisdom and learning, and to flourish. This consensus allows us to celebrate our differences without letting those often firmly and proudly held distinctions turn to violence. It allows us to communicate peacefully while still retaining our principled stand. It is possible in our society for two parties to exchange widely differing views always knowing that disagreements can be legitimately held without fear that those disagreements will lead to conflict.

Differences in customs and practices are often reflected in religious beliefs: what can and cannot be eaten, religious festivals and traditions, mores and standards of behaviour. With so many apparent differences, it may seem hard to find common ground, but the first step is to accept those differences because at their root are basic human characteristics: fear, love, envy, avarice, loneliness, uncertainty. Some people do not shake hands but bow courteously stemming from the basic fear of cleanliness and contamination; other people have a fear of the symbolic message of objects, others fear the perceived unclean nature of certain foods; while still others avoid touching animals which some may regard as their closest companions. We fear what we do not know or understand, but we are all able to smile, laugh and cry. We can all suffer from hunger and thirst in exactly the same way, and we can all enjoy celebrations of birthdays, festivals and fond memories.

What is at stake: fear of consensus, of crossing the divide, of reaching out? Britain allows for all differences, but what we must surely do is always call out the abuse of religion, the deliberate misinterpretation of classical religious teaching for political motives.

The British don't always take themselves too seriously, we allow mild teasing – even of our religions. The late Irish comedian, Dave Allen, often gently mocked the Catholic church on his TV show, but always with a twinkle in his eye. He would end his monologues with the phrase: May your god go with you, which seemed to cover every eventuality! To some Jesus Christ is the son of God, to others he was merely a prophet, one among many. For Catholics the eucharist and wine become the body and blood of Christ through transubstantiation, to Church of England followers it is just a celebration of the Last Supper, and the host and wine are unchanged. But whatever one believes we, in Britain, are all allowed to speak his name, portray him in images and, yes, even crack jokes about him and his followers without provoking a violent backlash. The key point is that is the way we behave in Britain. We don't force anyone to attend a religious service, we don't force anyone to dress in a particular way in churches. At the same time, we allow everyone to worship as they please, but that should never be a licence to criticise others with a different belief or who may be agnostic and therefore totally disagree with religion in all its guises.

Integration is an aim not reality, and a tolerant religion should be a key to that ambition not the obstacle. It is traditional for many followers of the Muslim faith, for instance, to insist that women wear full face coverings, but that is not the law in Britain and the worry is that it instantly creates a barrier. We communicate with our eyes and our facial expressions, and while Britons are regarded as a reserved race in general, we rely on being able to read people's faces to understand their true feelings. Nevertheless, unlike other nations we tolerate what some may think is discriminatory against women unless the women themselves voluntarily abide by those customs in their private lives.

Separation of men and women in synagogues and mosques is not unique to the Jewish or Muslim faiths. Out of habit and tradition women in Catholic churches in Ireland have followed the same practice, particularly in more rural communities, probably because the men stood around talking outside the church until the last moment before mass began. But the world is moving on. If women are ordained ministers of the Church of England – the first female chaplain to the Speaker of the House of Commons, the Rev Rose Hudson-Wilkin, was appointed in 2010 and succeeded by Patricia Hillas in 2019 – it shows that full emancipation is gathering pace. The first female bishop, the Rev Libby Lane, was elevated to the post of Bishop of Stockport in 2014 just a month after the change to canon law and 20 years after the first women became priests. Again, there is still resistance to the ordination of women in Britain, but that resistance is gradually fading except among the older traditionalists, and any such resistance is giving way to grudging acceptance. There was no hostility, no violence, just some heated rhetoric before canon law was changed. And that is the way change should come about.

Everyone has the right to freedom of religion throughout the United Kingdom, and that includes the right to convert to another religion or set of beliefs. It is regarded as a matter of private conscience. While the monarch is the Supreme Governor of the Church of England it is not always appreciated that before the coronation every monarch must swear an oath "to maintain and preserve inviably settlement of the Church of England, and the doctrine, worship, discipline, and government thereof, as by law established in England." In addition, all clergy of the Church of England must swear an oath of allegiance to the monarch, as do MPs, before they can take office.

While everyone in Britain is protected under Article 9 of the Human Rights to hold religious and non-religious beliefs which cannot be interfered with by the state, that right comes with a qualification of how one shows those beliefs – wearing a necklace with a cross or religious clothing – which protects the rights of others.

There is international recognition of this freedom of choice under a resolution adopted by the United Nations General Assembly under Article 18 of the International Covenant on Civil and Political Rights:

"Everyone shall have the right to freedom of thought, conscience and religion. This right shall include freedom to have or adopt a religion or belief of his choice, and freedom, by the individually or in community with others and in public or private, to manifest his religion or belief in worship, observance, practice or teaching."

Before we are accused of being hypocritical, such tolerance was not always practised in Britain. Jews were expelled in 1290 under Edward 1, anti-Catholicism began with Henry VIII and the Act of Supremacy in 1534 which cost the lives of Catholic martyrs, Mary Queen of Scots, regarded by her supporters as the rightful queen of England as a Catholic, was executed on the orders of her first cousin, Elizabeth 1. Archbishop Oliver Plunkett was the last Catholic to be executed in the country for "promoting the Roman faith" on charges of high treason for allegedly plotting an invasion by France in 1681. Charles 11 regretted his death but refused to pardon him for fear of anti-Catholic feelings in the country. Plunkett was canonised as a saint by Pope Paul VI in 1975.

Freedom of belief only sounds threatening to zealots who refuse to countenance any alternative to their point of view. Invariably their voices are raised and strident as they condemn all those who disagree to the point where they seek to impose their belief on whole communities governing what they eat and drink, what they teach, read and watch. That is not the sort of life most Britons want to lead. Freedom of belief means a freedom of choice, freedom to disagree, freedom to debate openly without fear of being accused of racism or being intolerant to others, without having to be so politically correct that any argument is reduced to meek acquiescence of every minority opinion for fear of causing offence where none is intended.

This has nothing to do with the law, with the Human Rights Act, or UN resolutions, it is all about how we in Britain choose to behave towards one another. You can have your beliefs but never force them on others, you can have your opinions but express them courteously and be prepared for polite disagreement. It is what the diplomats call protocol: diplomats have the freedom to travel even in hostile territories to represent their own countries. They are not trying to change the ways of their host nations, they are there to learn, to share understanding, to assist in trade negotiations and to ensure precisely that there are no hostilities between nations. Britain has an open-door policy to all legal visitors because by sharing other peoples' wisdom and culture we all benefit. It only goes wrong when someone believes that they know the true path to what might be called spiritual enlightenment. Nobody does.

Our Education

"Not a Social Experiment"

Great Britain stands high in lists of leading educational countries behind America. Our great universities attract students from around the world bringing with them valuable higher tuition fees (£28.8 billion per annum), our research and science are world renowned having produced 90 Nobel prize winners in chemistry, physics and medicine; our schools are generally well attended and led by dedicated teachers. And yet it is all under threat; standards are being eroded, the basic curriculum is being questioned and eventually the only losers will be the young people who have no say about the social experimentation. Why are we so determined to abandon our traditional aspirations to achieve the very best just to accommodate "in vogue" policies which later prove to be flawed? Where are these threats coming from and why do we take a world-class academic system for granted?

For the older generation the idea of questioning their teacher or their parents was unheard of for a variety of reasons, but respect for those in authority was perhaps foremost. Today's unpopular and uncomfortable notion of discipline permeated home life, school and the workplace, but that is being constantly challenged today; we are back to rights and responsibilities. Instead of doing what they are told, pupils in schools are increasingly challenging the authority of their teachers who sometimes are even physically threatened. According to government data, persistent disruptive behaviour is the most common reason for permanent exclusions and suspensions, and the highest rate of permanent exclusions is among pupils entitled to free school meals.

Everything starts at home. If a child believes there will be no retribution from their parents if they play truant, then they will be on the path to failure. If there is no parental support for headteachers punishing poor attendance or ill-discipline, then ultimately it will be the child who will pay the price. Among the highest groups repeatedly missing school are the traveller community and mixed-race pupils, the Chinese have the lowest rates of absence, and it is no coincidence that they had the highest number of students (40.7% in 2020/2021) at Britain's top universities.

Childhood resilience seems to be on the wain, perhaps because every child gets lavishly praised – Amazing! – for the most modest achievement, and admitting failure to come top of the class or first in the race is regarded as detrimental to a child's wellbeing. But it ill-prepares the child for life ahead which will be full of setbacks, rejection and pitfalls. The ability to pick oneself up and march on is being weaned out of our youth.

Everyone agreed that the enforced closure of schools during the Covid 19 pandemic was detrimental to the wellbeing of pupils, they missed the social interaction with their friends and, of course, they missed some two years of precious schooling – online teaching was never going to make up for the lost time. It put pressure on families who could not find or afford child minders, and mental health issues increased among children.

But Covid was beyond the control of academia, what isn't is the attempt to social engineer education at all levels for reasons of political correctness, perceived racism and social discrimination, the so-called Woke experience. The former vice chancellor of Cambridge University, Stephen Toope, speaking about the number of privately educated applicants, said: "I would say we have to keep making it very, very clear we are intending to reduce over time the number of people who are coming from independent school backgrounds." Happily, his comments were widely condemned, and he has since resigned from the university. Nevermind that some of those applicants may have been from deprived backgrounds who through sheer hard work and intelligence had won scholarships to attend private schools and would therefore be excluded under his proposed regime.

One Cambridge academic, Professor David Abulafia, a fellow of Gonville and Caius, went further and warned of a brain drain of the brightest students because admission policies were discriminating against "white, male and privileged" applicants. (*Daily Telegraph*,14 May 2022). This appeared to be confirmed by UCAS, the UK's admissions service, which reported later that disadvantaged pupils were being "put first" in the selection process.

Oxford and Cambridge Universities are at the pinnacle of the British education system, attracting the very brightest students, but by skewing the entrance qualification based on the school one attended rather than the grades one achieved, or worse because of the colour of one's skin or private background, can only do harm; in 2022 increasing numbers of pupils from independent schools were applying to the top US universities as Oxford and Cambridge appeared to focus on state school applicants.

Perhaps the key point there is hard work which alongside discipline is an uncomfortable concept. Katherine Moana Birbalsingh CBE is headteacher of a free school in Wembley called Michaela Community School, which she founded having experienced teaching at state schools in London. Dubbed by the media as 'the strictest headteacher in Britain', she supports traditional teaching methods saying that "education should be about teaching children knowledge, not learning skills." In 2010, addressing the Conservative Party Conference she spoke about "the chaos in the classroom." She demands high standards and discipline from her pupils, bans mobile phones, has warned against "indulging the bigotry of low expectations" and emphasises the importance of learning about British culture and Britishness, so pupils no longer feel excluded. Her results speak for themselves: Ofsted (Office for Standards in Education) judged her school to be "outstanding" and more than half of all GCSE grades were 7 or above.

Education is the pursuit of knowledge through inquiry and experiment. It is a child's natural instinct to ask "why". Why can't I do this? Why must I do that? It demands an answer which imparts knowledge. According to the Maltese proverb, a question is the sister of wisdom. The same questioning should extend throughout life. Why should a Shakespeare text be banned? (See Chapter 2.) What was he saying in his plays which was so offensive that a school dare not let a pupil's inquiring mind study it? And take it further, why should people be prevented from reading the Bible, the Koran or the Guru Granth Sahib, the Sikhs' sacred text? At the other extreme DH Lawrence's Lady Chatterley's Lover was condemned as being too salacious for decent eyes – today it barely qualifies as indecent. It is only by studying broadly that real understanding can be reached, which is not the same as agreement. The works of poets Philip Larkin and Wilfred Owen were removed from the GCSE curriculum by the OCR examination board and replaced with a more diverse group of authors – a move which was condemned by the Education Secretary at the time, Nadhim Zahawi, as "cultural vandalism". Education gives us the ability to understand another point of view, however, by being selective, even restrictive, in what we can study results only in narrowmindedness and bigotry.

If the curriculum is broad while retaining the basics of reading, writing and arithmetic any pupil at school will be prepared to progress with their further education, but stunt that growth with limited texts, politically correct lectures and misinterpretations, and the child will suffer, its mind corrupted by falsehoods and blackholes in their learning. And that is precisely what is happening in unregistered religious schools.

In some of these schools, for example Jewish Yeshiva schools, English is not even spoken, and academic subjects are not taught. OFSTED estimated in 2019 that a fifth of unregistered schools were faith schools – 36 Islamic, 18 Jewish and 12 Christian. (*BBC*, 9 May 2022). While we are blessed in this country with so much freedom to explore and debate and challenge, it is tragic that a minority seek to restrict the life chances of their children in this way. It is not that these freedoms of expression are being taken for granted so much as they are being wilfully, and in some cases illegally, ignored.

By law religious education (RE) must be taught in all British state schools, although evidence suggests that requirement is being loosely interpreted and not all secondary schools had formal RE lessons. But a broad curriculum should also include English, history (without a politically correct bias), mathematics, science and languages, art and design, technology and computing, music and physical education. As Nick Gibb MP, the former minister for schools' standards, wrote: "It is dangerous nonsense to believe that (critical thinking and problem-solving skills) can be developed without a foundation of knowledge and academic study." (*Daily Telegraph*, 24 August 2022)

The statutory national curriculum in England and Wales was introduced in 1988 (and in Northern Ireland in 1992) to ensure all children enjoyed the same level of education, which some may think was a little late in the day, but we now have a syllabus to follow which ensures that every pupil at least has the same opportunity and the same life chances. All the more reason to question why some communities deliberately choose to turn their backs on the opportunities that education has to offer.

The disruption of Covid 19 notwithstanding, the rigours of testing in examinations is just as important as it is in sport. Not everyone can come first in the race but that is not a reason to stop racing. We learn about losing, but we also learn about trying harder. Not everyone can be nuclear physicist but that is no reason not to study science, not everyone can be a concert pianist but that is no reason to stop practising and playing as best you can.

Exams are not meant to deflate a candidate's confidence they are designed to assess knowledge, to boost memory and to learn about the competitions ahead in life. And, of course, success breeds confidence to achieve greater things. A mountain climber is not satisfied having climbed one peak, they will always go in search of a higher mountain, a greater challenge.

Doing away with tests and examinations is the equivalent of dumbing down, not levelling up. It is being satisfied with the lowest common denominator. It is accepting a candidate for their background, their looks, their social history, even their gender not because they are the very best in the field. It may sound unfair, but then life is unfair, which is perhaps the first lesson to learn and the first challenge to overcome. Not everyone has the same ability, the same strengths, even the same looks, but everyone has their own personal gift which is the challenge for teachers to discover and to nurture.

Is the campaigning to bring an end to private education a policy of envy? Instead, should it not be a challenge to achieve the very best through diligence and hard work as demonstrated by the pupils of Katherine Moana Birbalsingh's Michaela Community School in London where they ask for no special treatment?

The private sector of independent schools educates some 6% of the UK's school population which is not many. However, the complaint always raised against these institutions is that because their pupils are privileged and their parents rich enough to pay the fees, they will have an unfair advantage in life: the class sizes will be smaller, the facilities will be greater and the distractions from their studies will be minimal, and therefore they are more likely to get better grades. Better grades result in greater access to the best universities which in turn lead to the most lucrative careers on graduation. In short, better life chances.

The answer is not easy or obvious but is surely not to abolish what is clearly delivering high quality education. The focus should be on improving the education in the state sector which can be achieved, not only through greater funding and smaller class sizes, but also by following the rigorous teaching discipline of the likes of Michaela Community School. Children have got to want to go to school where they know they will be safe and will learn to learn. They have got to have the support of their parents which in the most troubled neighbourhoods will be a challenge. Society itself must move on from looking enviously at what a tiny minority have, to building on what hundreds of thousands of families arriving in the country every year believe we have already got. We absolutely take for granted that we have free education and, in some cases, free school meals, which those playing truant wilfully ignore. The young girls in Afghanistan who have been forbidden even attending a school just because of their sex, would walk miles in all weathers for the same privilege. Such is their desire to learn that they are prepared to risk severe punishment and attend secret classes. One teacher was quoted as saying: "We do our best to do this secretly, but even if they arrest me and beat me, it's worth it." (*BBC Kabul,* 14 May 2022)

Privilege, therefore, is all about perspective. There is no doubt that the 6% privately educated children are privileged. It is right, even essential, that the state educated children should enjoy better teaching and better facilities, but the answer is not to destroy something that patently works well, rather it is to improve the rest. The reason that Chinese children are so diligent is because they are probably an only child. Their attitude is simple: to succeed, particularly when competition in so strong, they have got to work hard. Their parents will make any sacrifice to ensure they achieve high grades in school and university because they may in time become the only breadwinner in the family. Research shows that Chinese children succeed because they have a strong work ethic, putting in extra hours of study after school at home.

Just because one has gone to an independent sector school is no guarantee of success, and just because one has gone to a state school is no barrier to achieving one's ambitions. Both require application. The risk pupils in both systems take is not bothering to try, even rebelling against the discipline required. The risk an Afghan girl and her family take is severe, possibly physical danger for trying to learn; if some agency is prepared to bomb a school for daring to educate its children, then parents, teachers and children themselves must show real courage to turn up at the school gates or clandestine classroom. There are no free school meals, there are no extra curricula activities, there are no playground facilities, all of these we take for granted. Everything can be improved; it is just a question of one's starting point. Before we start tearing down patently excellent academic systems in a downward race to equality, we must treasure that excellence and seek to raise all standards, never being satisfied like the mountaineer climbing ever higher.

The curriculum should be all-encompassing with nothing off limits and everything subject to rigorous academic, not violent, challenge. Libraries should be full of the greatest works of literature and science, not confiscated and burned for danger of posing enlightened but forbidden opinion. Above all, no one should be excluded just because of social background or race. British education offers all these things and is recognised the world over for its freedom of thought and defends the right to express those opinions, courteously but firmly, at all costs. The Office for Students warned, however, that "lawful views are being stifled" in some universities. Andrea Jenkyns, the higher education minister, said: "Universities and colleges must be places that champion debate and diversity of thought and this government has warned of the chilling effect of censorship on our campuses." (*Daily Telegraph*, 15 July 2022)

The alternative is no better than the streets of Afghanistan where fear of expression stalks every corner, where knowledge is regarded as a dangerous threat to the political order and where teaching is a crime punishable by beating or worse.

As the Sanskrit proverb about knowledge and power says: *"There is no comparison between a king and a scholar, as the king is celebrated only in his country, whereas a scholar is celebrated everywhere."*

Our English Language

"A Universal Tongue"

What a gift to the world! To be fair, of course, it didn't come as a ready-made package indeed we should be in part grateful to invading German tribes – the Jutes, Angles and Saxons. The true Englishman may claim to be of long-standing Anglo-Saxon stock but that really means they are part German. However, like every language, it evolves and the English we speak today has developed over the centuries, mixed with Celtic dialects, Latin and Greek, long forgotten versions of how people spoke, before transforming into something recognisable with the Norman invasion in 1066; even though French became the language used in royal circles until the start of the Hundred Years War between France and England in the late Middle Ages when to speak French was regarded as disloyal. Indeed, it was not until the Tudors that English became the official language of the royal court.

But English, like Britain itself, welcomes all, absorbs influences from around the world and as a result helps billions of people in every country prosper in all walks of life. The joy of English today is its universality and richness making it the fastest growing language.

Nothing could be further from the truth than the sophistry of the argument that the English language supports the claim of "white superiority" as asserted in an Open University training course for academics in 100 UK universities in 2022. The module stated: "Along with religion, politics, laws and customs, white superiority is embedded in the linguistic and cultural psychology of the English language. Consequently, given the global reach of the English language, the assumption of white hegemony has been covertly weaved into the consciousness of white people, black people and people of colour."

The assertion was swiftly dismissed as "ignorant" by Dr Zareer Masani, a historian of the British Empire, who said: "It is an alarming sign of how wokedom is taking over academia. It's unhistorical, it's ignorant, and it's illiterate. It completely ignores non-white contributions to the English language and totally dismisses the role of people ranging from Achebe to

Rushdie who have enriched English by writing in English."
(Daily Telegraph, 16 June 2022)

Just how has English become one of the dominant languages of the world, the dominant second language of the world, the language of Air Traffic Control and of more than half the users of the Internet?

In truth the British Empire had a significant part to play but was it such a detrimental part? Did "foreigners" suffer for being made to learn English in the schools and universities the Empire established?

Modern India, and for that matter, modern Britain, have much to be thankful for that fact that the English language was encouraged by the powerful East India Company (EIC). Where would the NHS be today without the input from Indian surgeons, consultants, doctors and nurses? Where would the business community or the judiciary be without the influence of the Asian community many of whom trace their families back to the days of the "Raj"?

Professor Lalvani writes in his book, *The Making of India*: "In 1854 the EIC issued a dispatch for a modern state education system in India; the following decades would see important strides in government support of an egalitarian state education provision. The English language proliferated and became the principal medium for training in the sciences; this legacy endures today. A single language of education allowed a cohesive higher education system, with independent learning institutions across the Indian subcontinent facilitated and united by the strong shared bond of a common language of science." (*The Making of India – The Untold Story of British Enterprise* – Bloomsbury 2016).

Where would the Pony Clubs of the world be without their gymkhanas – gym from the Hindi *gend* meaning ball, and *khana* from the Persian meaning home or compartment? What would the riders of the world be wearing without jodhpurs, from the late 19th century and named after garments worn by Indian men? And where would people in bungalows be living whose origins stem from the Gujarati *bangalo* and the Hindi *bangla* meaning low thatched house. All examples of international influence, or one might say: e.g. (*exempli gratia*, Latin *exemplum* meaning example and *gratia* meaning grace.)

The origins of most English words are from Latin or Greek then evolved through French and German. English is something of a magpie language, if it doesn't have a word, it steals it from another language often German – kindergarten. In a world where someone's gender seems to be increasingly flexible, some advocates of a sexless society may be interested to know that the origins of the word 'girl' was 'gor' in German which was used to describe children of either sex (male or female).

The etymology of words merits a lifetime of study but to suggest that English implies white superiority is plainly nonsensical (French origin *nonsens*), or one might even say a hazardous (Arabic origin *al zahr* meaning dice used in gambling) argument to make. The so-called loanwords from other languages which we use in everyday parlance are truly international: banana (Senegal), chimpanzee (Congo), trek (South Africa), cot (India), etc., (etcetera, *et* meaning *and*, *cetera* meaning *rest* in Latin).

However, there should be no shame about defending the spoken word, clear diction and good grammar where it helps improve communication which is why English is the official language of Air Traffic Control; what could be more dangerous than a misunderstanding at 36,000 feet? Equally newscasters are by definition communicators, but here there is a tendency for some broadcasters to prove their diversity by including news presenters and correspondents speaking with broad regional accents. The implication being that only an Irish, Welsh or Scottish reporter can deliver a news report with authenticity from Ireland, Wales or Scotland. They may be the best in their field but if their accent is so broad that the message is lost or is a distraction, then the exercise in diversity has failed.

To speak what is still known as the Queen's English is regarded as old fashioned, too upper class, too superior, but to speak correctly should not be sneered at nor taken for granted. The French regard correct pronunciation particularly highly and defend corruption of their language vigorously. The Académie Française was established by Cardinal Richelieu in 1635 tasked with preserving the French language in its purest form; in fact, a particular complaint of theirs is the influence of 'Franglais', the corruption of French by English words and phrases. The Academy publishes the official dictionary of the language.

Brexit caused much bad blood, so much so that moves were made to remove English as one of the so-called Procedural Languages of the European Union, along with French and German, which are used to publish all official documents. It remains as one of the 24 recognised languages.

Such is the dominance of English in more than 60 countries that it has become the number one language of business for easier communication. Invariably people like visitors to try a few words of the local language before demonstrating their superior knowledge of English.

According to Harvard Business Review (2012) English is undoubtedly the language of business communication: "Ready or not, English is now the global language of business. More and more multinational companies are mandating English as the common corporate language dash Airbus, Daimler-Chrysler, Fast Retailing, Nokia, Renault, Samsung, SAP, Technicolor, and Microsoft in Beijing to name a few – in an attempt to facilitate communication and performance across geographically diverse functions and business endeavors."

The reality is we are living and working in a globally diverse society, and one never knows who might be at the end of a Zoom call, which country they are working in and what the native language might be. English, spoken by two billion people must be the answer in order to get the deal done. In short, everyone in business is expected to be fluent in English not as a sign of superiority, but as an essential to communicate with the majority. What is sometimes surprising, and impressive, in TV news reports is how many ordinary men and women in the street – the Vox Pops – are able to be interviewed in fluent English. How many people in the UK could speak to a reporter in French, Spanish or German, three of the other most common languages?

English has also developed into the primary language of science from Latin in Europe or Arabic in the Middle East; indeed, the very word "scientist" (from the Latin *scientia)* was coined by the theologian and historian of science, the Rev William Whewell, only in the 19th century, before that the study of nature was conducted by 'nature philosophers'.

Gradually the importance of peer review meant English became the *'lingua franca"*, the common language. However, that only became the case around the time of World War 1 and with the rise in importance of the United States in science. Quite how long that will last is open to debate with China's research output ahead of the rest of the world's. Perhaps in time all scientific papers will be in Mandarin, but for the immediate and maybe long-term future English will remain the language of science and of business.

A single language for science in particular presents obvious disadvantages for non-native speakers not only in understanding lectures and reading other research papers, but in presenting their own findings in all-English journals. Some argue that this means vital scientific knowledge can be missed, even valuable folklore. Writing in The Atlantic magazine, Adam Huttner-Koros reported: "Knowledge that isn't produced via traditional academic research methods can still have scientific value – indigenous tribes in Indonesia, for example, knew from their oral histories how to recognise the signs of an impending earthquake, enabling them to flee to higher ground before the 2004 tsunami hit." (*The Atlantic, The Hidden Bias of Science's Universal Language,* 21 August 2015)

Sometimes research published in a foreign language is simply not picked up as was the case in January 2004 when

Chinese scientists reported their concerns about the deadly H5N1 virus affecting the Asian bird population. Their urgent warning about the possibility of the virus jumping to humans only appeared in a Chinese veterinary magazine and wasn't noticed by the World Health Organisation until the following August when it was swiftly translated into English for a wider audience. (*Smithsonian Magazine,* January 2017)

Now, of course, the very meaning of common English words is changing as a result of the highly flexible and inventive social media. Tweets were the sounds birds made, post came through your letterbox delivered every day by the postman and streams were babbling brooks trickling leisurely through the woods. Not anymore.

Surely nothing in linguistics can match the speed at which the language of social media is evolving. The development and changing fashions of acronyms move at a blistering pace; just as the 'grown ups' master the meaning of OMG it is dropped from the 'lexicon' of the ever-younger users. They themselves are experimenting and adapting to see what will catch on particularly with the 'influencers' who dictate so much of what the younger, faster minds choose to adopt and believe.

It took centuries for the English language the world is speaking today to evolve; it is taking mere moments for the language of social media to have developed into the new 'lingua franca'. English language courses have been forced to recognise this new way of communicating because all the traditional rules of grammar and sentence construction are abandoned when you chose to send a 280 character 'tweet'. To the uninitiated 'grown up' who may still be struggling to master a smart phone, it is a new foreign language. Not only are the words different, even meaningless, but words are increasingly being replaced with symbols – the emojis which convey, as the word suggests, a host of different emotions. A smiling face is all one needs to send in response to a long, happy message. It is quicker which is precisely the reaction the sender of the message wants. There are downsides, of course, because failing to send an instantaneous thumbs up symbol to a photograph can cause anxiety – why am I being ignored. That can be shrugged off by mature users, but impressionable children who do not feel "liked" by their classmates can all too easily become depressed. Social media has a lot to answer for socially.

The scope for misinterpretation or misunderstanding in this world of tweets is a worry because increasingly it has replaced the need for a normal conversation. A tweet can only convey so much, it has no tone or inflexion. It is too short to be able to express oneself clearly and once fired into the Twittersphere cannot be recalled or explained with a "Sorry, you missed my point, what I was trying to say was…"

The young masters of the medium today are much more inclined to send a tweet than to have a phone conversation and those that do talk might as well be speaking a foreign language as far as their parents are concerned.

The on-line language of social media has spilled over into everyday conversation which, of course, is the way language evolves, but whether the English language is richer is open to debate. The spoken word is becoming as casual and ungrammatical as those short, sharp 280-character messages. The ability to construct a sentence of any length is being lost, certainly without the interjection of "like" between every other word. There was a time when members of parliament would be expected to stand up and deliver a well-rounded speech without referring to their notes, powerful and persuasive enough to galvanise the country to face Nazi tyranny, but that oratorical skill has been lost. And maybe that doesn't matter if the words they deliver are just as compelling, but language is all about communicating to win an argument or just to impart some information. If one can't speak clearly and effectively the information will be as garbled as a misunderstood tweet.

The Oxford English Dictionary, the arbiter of acceptable words – itself only available online – allows for the new words spilling over from the Internet, but for now we are some way from abandoning the pleasure and power of a language which dominates the world in an inclusive sense because it enables countless millions of people to understand one another. There need be no resistance to the technological adaptation of a language which for many is the bedrock of all their understanding, so long as the language which evolved methodically and logically through Latin and Greek, French, German and Arabic into a rich method of communication, of literature and poetry is not lost by being casually taken for granted.

Our Benign Climate

"Temperate but Changing"

Whether it's raining cats and dogs, or like a mad dog and an Englishman you're out in the midday sun, the British climate has it all, making it our favourite topic of conversation. If you're taking your geography exam the UK's climate would best be described as temperate, the Köppen Climate Classification calls it a subtropical oceanic climate, but we all know it tends to be warmer and drier in the south and wetter and cooler in the north. Until that is climate change intervenes and presents us with unseasonal heatwaves and snowstorms across the whole country, then, of course, we complain bitterly about how difficult it is to sleep through the hot nights or wonder whether the rain is ever going to stop.

So, what is benign about our weather and what place does it have in a book about taking our realm for granted? One word: fragility.

Our usual weather patterns offer something for everyone. You can ski in the mountains of Scotland and bask in the sunshine on the south coast, you can fish for salmon on the Don or surf off the coast of Cornwall, you can trek across the mountains of Wales and marvel at the Mountains of Mourne in Northern Ireland as they sweep down to the sea, or laze on the Norfolk Broads, and all of this in one United Kingdom. Despite such riches we are in a hurry to race to the airport to soak up the sun on some foreign beach. As the daytime and night-time temperatures broke all UK records in the summer of 2022 reaching over 40 degrees, it seemed reasonable to ask why.

The geography of our land merits a detour because it contributes so much to our climate.

First of all, the United Kingdom of Great Britain and Northern Ireland is an island nation – including some six thousand large and small islands – so the seas which surround us, the Atlantic to the north and west, and the North Sea to the east play a crucial part. Technically the Channel Islands are not part of the British Isles from a geographical point of view because they are not part of the same archipelago, but they are every bit as British as Cheddar Cheese and the White Cliffs of Dover.

We have mountains to the north and west, with the Pennines running down the spine and lowlands to the south and east, we have the mighty Thames, the Severn, the Great Ouse, the Tweed and the Tay, and countless more rivers wending their way through our land. They all have their part to play in our environment which we most certainly do take for granted.

Great Britain alone cannot change what is happening to the global climate, but we can make a difference in our own small way. No-one would suggest that our country   is particularly dry, for instance, despite intermittent water restrictions and hosepipe bans, but we should take care of our rivers, and not waste or pollute the water. The Environment Agency warned in 2019 that within 25 years England would not have enough water to meet demand, mostly as a result of climate change. James Bevan, head of the Agency, described it as an "existential threat". We cannot stop the population growing, but we can control how much water we use, and we can take care of the rivers. The seas that surround us are plentiful if they are not over-fished and the land has the potential to feed us if it is protected and nurtured; more than one desalination plant for a land surrounded by water would make a difference. Our natural world is one of the big draws for tourists and holiday makers, they should remember to leave the beauty that attracted them in the first place in the same condition they found it.

Overall, the UK was 0.8 degrees warmer in 2022 than it was over the previous decade. Some may say we are blessed by the Gulf Stream which brings with it warmer air from the Caribbean and the North Atlantic Drift which draws in warm water from the South Atlantic. We are a truly lucky realm in this regard. Some might go so far as to say that the moderating influence of the Atlantic Ocean has encouraged the stoicism that used to be a particularly English characteristic.

If our benign weather has all the ingredients required for a prosperous agricultural industry there are other threats: shortage of supplies, encroachment of building into agricultural land, the rights and wrongs of the use of insecticides, the cost of organic farming, and then when all the right ingredients come together for a bumper harvest that unexpected turn in the weather may strike. Too much sun on parched soil and too little rain, and the crops die. Too much rain and too little sun, and the crops fail to ripen. A farmer's lot can be a tough one.

However, we can support the hardworking farmers by buying local produce and only eating seasonal food, not demanding year-round bananas and oranges, shipping avocadoes across the world for our salads, insisting on increasingly exotic foods from distant lands. In fact, because our climate is warming, we can benefit from the rising temperatures by growing what could only be found in the heat of French and Spanish summers. The British wine industry is but one example where sparkling wines now compete in all but name with the vineyards of Champagne.

Assuming no-one doubts that the climate is warming we can at least be prepared for what is coming and adapt. The Maritime Climate Change Impacts Partnership (MCCIP) in its latest assessment (Report Card 2020) outlined what was at stake:

- There is clear evidence that warming seas, reduced oxygen, ocean acidification and sea-level rise are already affecting UK coasts and seas, with impacts on plankton, fish, birds and mammals

- Coastal flooding is likely to get worse, due to the combined effects of higher sea level rises than previously thought and more extreme rainfall

- Fisheries productivity in some UK waters has been negatively impacted by ocean warming and historical overexploitation, emphasising the need for sustainable management of stocks that accounts for climate change impacts

- Impacts of climate change have already been observed at a range of coastal heritage sites due to increased erosion, flooding, weathering or decay.

"This report collates important new evidence which highlights how climate change has already affected UK coasts and seas, and the ways it will continue to do so in the coming decades. This information is crucial to not only help develop adaptation measures and management actions to support vulnerable marine life and habitats, but also to help UK industries and society prepare for and adapt to these far-reaching marine climate impacts." (UK *Centre for Ecology & Hydrology*)

Our flooding may never be as extreme as what they must endure in countries like Bangladesh, but as the MCCIP report warns low lying land, particularly on the east coast, will in time have to be abandoned to the sea; there is only so much one can do to prevent coastal erosion and rising sea levels. We can build our defences but there are physical and economic limits to what can be done and is worth doing. Inland, where we have witnessed rivers bursting their banks and flooding whole neighbourhoods, the worst effects can to a certain extent be prevented by not building on flood plains and by maintaining the countryside further upstream, by planting more trees and working with nature not against it. If we strip away the land upstream there is nothing to capture and redirect heavy rainfall.

A study by Exeter University found that when they reintroduced beavers in Devon, and they were allowed to build their dams, the incidence of flooding downstream was reduced and boosted wildlife. (*BBC* 17 February 2020) The warning signals have been there for some time. The UN Environment Programme reported in 2007 in its Global Environment Outlook: "Imagine a world in which environmental change threatens people's health, physical security, material needs and social cohesion. This is a world beset by increasingly intense and frequent storms, and by rising sea levels. Some people experience extensive flooding, while others endure intense droughts. Species extinction occurs at rates never before witnessed. Safe water is increasingly limited, hindering economic activity. Land degradation endangers the lives of millions of people. This is the world today."

Net Zero targets are what the world sought to achieve when they came together in Glasgow in November 2021 for the COP26 summit, billed as the 'last chance saloon' to save the planet. But that was before the Russian invasion of Ukraine and the crisis in fuel supplies as a result of which countries were forced to look again at their ambitious targets and explored the unthinkable of reviving mothballed coal fired power stations and exploring new oil fields to make up the shortfall from Russian oil and gas supplies. Fossil fuels were once again acceptable in times of a geopolitical crisis, at least for the immediate short term and the moratorium on fracking, the process of pumping high pressure liquid into subterranean rocks to release gas and oil, was being reconsidered. They have been fracking successfully (and without the feared earthquakes) in America which, by 2017, was producing 67 percent of the nation's natural gas and some 50 percent of the oil, according to the US Energy Information Administration. In the same way as there is plenty of water on earth, there is plenty of oil but much of it may be too difficult or too expensive to extract.

The alternative, of course, is renewable energy and Britain is well placed to take advantage of the technologies available. We have sufficient sun to make solar panels viable, and wind particularly offshore to make windfarms highly effective. Our climate, it seems, has it all, perhaps it comes down to the balance between energy and aesthetics. There is nothing beautiful about acres of solar panels spreading across once arable fields, and the sight of wind turbines spoiling distant views of the horizon can hardly be described as attractive; it seems the birds don't like them either, and they may even confuse the sonar system of whales.

One estimate suggested that it would require 23,000 square kilometres of land (10% of the UK) for solar and windfarms to produce enough energy to replace oil. (www.carboncommentary.com) The report concluded that full decarbonisation using renewables was possible, but in whose backyard would these turbines and panels be sited?

So, we have the technology, and we have the weather to make a difference, it is just a question of how we choose to use them. Nuclear power, which is unaffected by the weather of course, is another option which already produces more than 18% of the country's electricity needs, but the pros and cons of nuclear power are another story.

For now, we must accept that our weather patterns are changing, the extremes of hot and cold will be greater and more frequent, but for the UK an increase of 0.8 degrees remains benign while the impact of rising sea levels and erosion will inevitably, in due course, be felt. We can help ourselves to a certain extent by a wise use of finite resources, by wise building programmes, by working with nature, by building more reservoirs, by repairing leaking pipes and by adapting our lifestyles to suit our climate. Perhaps it will not always remain benign, but we are lucky to live in a temperate climate, wafted by warm south westerly winds for the most part, and to have a country with the variety of weather that allows us to pick and choose either where we live or holiday.

The answer to the question does our benign weather have a place in such a book is assuredly yes. It defines our moods when the sun shines or the rain falls, and we have both in our varying seasons. There is only rarely a prolonged drought and only relatively brief, harsh winters both of which are reflected in our countryside, the animals which thrive here and the waters which surround us. We have rugged coastlines and sandy beaches; we have forests and fields teeming with wildlife and we have a duty to protect and preserve it all working with nature before it turns against us. As the climate changes so too will our landscape and all of our natural world; our very weather is fragile, we take it for granted at our own peril.

Our People

"An Evolving Species"

If Great Britain is not multicultural, as David Cameron asserted (Chapter 3) then we are certainly multi-cultured. But does that really define the British people? The typical "Brit", by which most foreigners would be thinking of an Englishman, has a stiff upper lip, is diffident and reserved to the point of shyness and probably drinks too much tea, or if they're at a football match too much beer when any such inhibitions miraculously disappear. But the melting pot, which the United Kingdom of nearly 60 million people is rapidly turning into, is much more complex.

Race is an issue because the assumption is that the country is being "over-run by foreigners', although the according to the latest statistics 87% of the people in the UK are white, 13% are black, Asian, Mixed or Other Ethnic group. Hardly over-run, however it all depends on where you live; the most diverse region of England and Wales is London, and the capital has the smallest percentage of White British people (44.9%) of all cities. People from the White Ethnic group were more likely to live in the South East. (www.gov.uk).

The full list of the ethnic groups living in our country is long:

Asian or Asian British

- Indian
- Pakistani
- Bangladeshi
- Chinese
- Any other Asian background

Black, Black British, Caribbean or African

- Caribbean
- African
- Any other Black, Black British, or Caribbean background

Mixed or multiple ethnic groups

- White and Black Caribbean
- White and Black African

- White and Asian
- Any other Mixed or multiple ethnic background

White

- English, Welsh, Scottish, Northern Irish or British
- Irish
- Gypsy or Irish Traveller
- Roma
- Any other White background

Other ethnic groups

- Arab
- Any other ethnic group

As most of us (81.5% of the general population) live in towns and cities as opposed to 18.5% in rural locations, our view on life, or the direction of travel the country is taking, can be skewed. If we live in Newham in London, for example, which has the lowest percentage of the white ethnic group (29%) of any local authority, then you may be inclined to believe as a white person that the country is definitely being "over-run by foreigners." And yet, of course, many of your neighbours may be second or third generation "Brits", and importantly consider themselves to be British.

What are the stereotypical characteristics of the native English, Irish, Scottish, and Welsh people?

Apart from his love of tea and beer, it is generally assumed the English like to queue, apologise at every opportunity, they are reserved and had a profound admiration and love for Her Majesty the Queen. The English love their sport, even if they are not always very good at it, and it is assumed that an Englishman living in the country (by which we mean countryside) will love his dog above all else.

The Irish have a soft lilting accent in the South, and something a bit sharper in the North, they are known for potatoes, Guinness and a good "craic" (partying), they are laid back and fiercely loyal, particularly in the North where the majority resist all attempts to revert to one united Ireland.

Scotland is famous for its Highlands, haggis, whisky, tartans and bagpipes. A true Scot is proud and again fiercely loyal some, currently in the minority, even to the point of demanding independence. (The Scottish Nationalist Party leader and First Minister, Nicola Sturgeon, called for a second referendum to be held in 2023, 55% of Scots having voted against in September 2014.)

The Welsh love their language and their singing, which, combined with rugby talent, make formidable opponents. They too have an independent streak, but no-one seriously expects them to break away from the United Kingdom.

So much for the original natives of Britain (although few are of genuine Ancient Briton stock), but into the melting pot we have already absorbed those who trace their own family roots from around the globe, and they are today every bit as British as anyone else born and bred in the country. Their skin may be a different colour but when they speak with a Scottish burr, they run Scottish businesses and they have only known life in Glasgow, Edinburgh or Aberdeen, they are true 'Brits", and it would be foolish and ill-judged to take them for granted.

The problem for the British people, as we have noted, is that while we have a cornucopia of ethnic blends in our islands, we do not have a blend in our lives. On the whole we are prepared to get along, but don't expect us to party together. The divide which the latest census reveals is that people want to live with their own kind. It may, in truth, be to do with deep seated racism among "whites" but it is also a factor of Asians, Pakistanis, Bangladeshis, Arabs, Africans preferring to be with their own 'people'. They dress the same way, the eat the same food, they celebrate the same way, they worship the same way and at home they speak their own language.

It will take time, decades, possibly longer, but the people of Britain will evolve into one homogenous race, hopefully enjoying the very best characteristics of each. It didn't take long for curry to become at least as popular as fish and chips, our popular music draws its inspiration from across the globe and there is no longer the strict taboo of inter-marrying; the young, one might say, are leading the way.

All the benefits of this nation will continue to draw people from every corner of the globe until eventually we cease to talk about ethnicity in our census reports; we may still have English, Irish, Scottish and Welsh geographical divisions but physically much will have changed, although the national character traits may well persist much as the accents have been readily adopted by our visitors. Down the centuries the country has absorbed and assimilated even the most hostile newcomers; we seem to have taken the best they have to offer and made them our own and the same will inevitably happen with our appearance.

In the meantime, what should not be taken for granted is the natural tolerance of the British people as they are today. The British may be "easy going" or "anything for a quiet life" but eventually the lion in us stirs. When Argentina invaded the Falkland Islands in 1982, the country was galvanised into action to take them back and then the military returned to its slumbers, mission accomplished. Until that is when Ukraine was invaded by Putin's forces; the head of the British Army, Gen Sir Patrick Sanders, warned all ranks and our allies in June 2022 that we must now be "capable of … defeating Russia." (*Chapter 5*). His warning echoed by Ben Wallace, the Defence Secretary, who urged the Treasury to find more money to invest in defence. (*Daily Telegraph,* 28 June 2020).

What is it about our people that, even as a small island nation, we feel obliged to take on the bigger international bullies? What is it in our nature that we choose to speak out for what is right and be prepared to take a lead? Not every European country was quite so quick to denounce Putin's aggression in Ukraine, to push for tough economic sanctions which would have severe economic consequences for our country and to be first to offer military support as soon as it was requested by President Volodymyr Zelensky.

The bulldog spirit, tenacity in the face of impossible odds, came to symbolise Britain most obviously during World War II when Winston Churchill, who looked uncannily like a bulldog, seemed to epitomise stubborn determination against Nazi Germany. And in World War I the cartoon character of John Bull standing proudly with a bulldog by his side, urged every man to do his duty.

There is undoubtedly a stubborn streak about the British character, a British tourist abroad always looks like a "Brit" probably because they refuse to adapt to what they perceive to be foreign ways, never bother trying to learn the local language, never being too adventurous tasting the local food and tending to travel in groups without risking something more off the beaten track.

But then these sweeping caricatures are immediately confounded by the (often) English eccentric who defies convention in dress, in habits and travel. In history they have been the pioneers who have risked all by exploring undiscovered lands. Some have gone completely native like DH Lawrence, "Lawrence of Arabia", the British army officer and writer who fought in the Arab Revolt against the Ottoman Empire (1916-1918). As Edith Sitwell wrote: "Eccentricity exists particularly in the English because of that peculiar and satisfactory knowledge of infallibility that is the hallmark and the birthright of the British nation." (*The English Eccentrics,* Edith Sitwell – *Pallas Athene, 1933)*

Infallibility, yes, if one takes the Battle of Hastings in 1066 as the last successful invasion of Britain, but self-confidence is probably more applicable in the modern world and that stems from the one inescapable factor which is class. There is a pecking order in the UK which refuses to go away – upper, middle and lower class. It has nothing to do with wealth because what we call the aristocracy who once ruled over all they surveyed have by and large fallen on hard times. The stately homes of England, celebrated in song by Noel Coward, have either been turned into hotels or opened up to the masses to visit and pay for the upkeep. Some have been turned into zoos and others into film sets to show how the aristocrats once used to live and 'held the upper hand." However, it really doesn't matter how impoverished a peer of the realm has become, he is still upper class, confident of his rightful (if forgotten) place in society and entitled to any whims and eccentricities he cares to exhibit. None of which matters a jot if one is wealthy enough to buy a dilapidated stately home because one has done well in business – but it doesn't make one upper class. If you don't speak properly (the Queen's English) and you don't know how to hold a knife and fork, nothing will enable you to climb the class ladder.

One might think that with the influx of so many 'foreigners' such distinctions would be diluted, but far from it as those visitors bring their own class distinctions. Indians have long had a very rigid hierarchy and, while there may no longer be a taboo about an English person (a *gora*) marrying an Indian bride, among Indians themselves there is the strict caste system divide which can be traced back to the Rig Vedic Period (1700-1000 BC). The structure developed into four classes, or castes, known as *chaturvarnas*. Brahmins, or priests, were at the top, below them were the Kshatriyas, who were above the Vaishyas, who in turn were above the Shudras or Untouchables. The Shudras role was to do all the menial tasks for their superiors. Another word for Shudra is Dalit which means 'the oppressed' and is used by them to emphasise how poorly they are treated in Indian society. It is said that one can distinguish a caste simply by the way women wear their saris. As the late author and broadcaster, Kailash Puri, wrote: "Not knowing a Dalit from a Brahmin, Britain has been a lifeline to the untouchables who, with the right opportunity, have made a success of their lives in the country because they are not treated as inferior." *(The Myth of UK Integration,* Kailash Puri – Whittles Publishing 2012).

It is said that more than 300 languages are spoken in London alone but for every language there is probably a mini ghetto of people from individual nations, all determined to better themselves and their families but separate from each other. The British who left Britain to enrich themselves overseas – it is estimated that 3 million emigrated between 1853 and 1880 alone – were no better at integrating in countries like India. Writing about the Indian Raj, Somerset Maugham, noted: "Even the working-class British women who are nowhere near the intelligence of Indian women kept them at arm's length."

Clearly what we mustn't do is take one another for granted. While people may be speaking 300 different languages in London, at some point during the day they probably all exchange a word or two of English. We shouldn't be living in parallel worlds, as Kailash Puri said: "Moving and breathing in the same space but effectively invisible to one another." For better or worse we are one nation made up of a multitude of different cultures but with the gift of a common language to help us communicate. Talking is always the first step towards reaching an understanding among peoples and we must surely be able to become closer to one another if we are living in the same country regardless of our ethnic backgrounds, home countries, and our family heritage. Britain's history proves that it can absorb the very best of every culture and that is what makes the people of Britain unique in the world, and this land a lucky realm.

The characteristics of the Englishman, the Irishman, the Scotsman and the Welshman may not change radically as a result of their new compatriots from overseas, but they most assuredly will evolve and probably for the better. The stiff upper lip of the Englishman may become a little less reserved, while the Scott who has always been mildly suspicious of any interloper into his highland territory will learn to adapt, even to a turban wearing Sikh who brings a canny business sense to an already canny Scot.

Where the people of Britain draw the line among all cultures is in the delicate area of marriage; it happens but so rarely that it is noticeable. It is one thing to do business with an Arab, a Pakistani or a Kurd just to use three examples, however it is quite another matter to allow one's daughter or son to marry outside one's own caste. While such ingrained distinctions remain, it will always be difficult to talk about one nation, one people, but that is inevitably what every nation becomes overtime. What we cannot forget are all the riches which our multi-cultured nation possesses thanks in no small part to the very rich diversity of all our people.

There is diversity on our screens and in our advertisements because that is what the law of the land demands, but it will take some time for those fictions to translate into real life. As we all know, organisations like our NHS could simply not operate without the skill and support of so many different people from all walks of life and from overseas. But at the end of the working day where do they all go and who do they relax with if not people from their own multi-cultured background? When we talk about our people, we mean all our people who make up our United Kingdom. In time perhaps we will become be a multicultural as opposed to a multi-cultured society, one where we are not astonished, or even suspicious, if someone who looks a little different to us greets us in the street as we pass by. It is not a very English thing to do, but perhaps our reserve can be gently broken down by the natural friendship of another people.

The Commonwealth

"Unity in Diversity"

The Commonwealth of Nations, to give it its full title, is under threat as much as our education and our democracy. The questions being asked are is it relevant and even is it necessary. Somehow people, one suspects, feel mildly ashamed of the Commonwealth, once known as the British Commonwealth of Nations before the 'British' was dropped in 1949 as it smacked too much of Empire. While the Queen remained as Head of the Commonwealth it was untouchable out of respect to her personally, but now she is no longer with us, although Prince Charles was unanimously voted as her 'designated successor' to the post which is not hereditary, the gaps in loyalty to the concept may emerge.

The British politician and future prime minister, Lord Roseberry, recognised in 1884 that, with the process of decolonisation of the Empire, countries would achieve their independence resulting in what he called a "Commonwealth of Nations". His foresight proved correct and in 1931 under the Statute of Westminster the association was formed with the founding five members – the United Kingdom, Canada, the Irish Free State, Newfoundland, and the Union of South Africa.

At the time of writing there are 56 independent countries in the Commonwealth from Africa and Asia, to the Americas, Europe and the Pacific. Two were never part of the British Empire – Mozambique (a Portuguese colony) and Rwanda (first German then Belgian) They include some of the largest and smallest states, each one with an equal voice, and include 2.5 billion people or nearly a third of the world's population, 60 per cent of whom are under the age of 30. The King is only head of state in 15 of the countries. Most have become republics, but, like India the first to declare independence, have chosen to remain in the Commonwealth. The most recent was Barbados which removed the Queen as its head of state in 2021 but also remains in the organisation. It was Jawaharlal Nehru, India's first Prime Minister, who wanted India to remain a member of the Commonwealth on becoming a Republic in 1950, who came up with the idea of recognising the British monarch as the Commonwealth's symbolic head, thus paving the way for other former colonies to follow suit as the independence movement gathered pace in the 1950s and 1960s. The Commonwealth has only had three Heads, King George VI, Queen Elizabeth II and now King Charles III. Apart from being a very large organisation with shared values of democracy, human rights and the rule of law, what is the point of the Commonwealth?

Her Majesty said in her Christmas Day broadcast in 1953 that she envisioned the Commonwealth as "an entirely new conception – built on the highest qualities of the Spirit of Man, friendship, loyalty, and the desire for freedom and peace." Qualities which today are sorely needed. One might, for instance, question where loyalty lies when Liverpool football fans deem it acceptable to boo during the playing of their country's national anthem at the FA Cup Final in 2022. An insignificant occurrence in the grand scheme of things but an indication of the depths to which some will stoop. The Commonwealth by contrast throws a collective arm around all its members and while some choose to appoint their own heads of state, they also choose to remain loyal to its ethos. The public demonstration by countless Commonwealth leaders at the Queen's Platinum Jubilee celebrations in 2022 spoke volumes. They all knew perfectly well that the monarch they were honouring would not remain indefinitely, but they equally understood the value and strength of a global, united family which the Commonwealth uniquely represents. And that is the point of the Commonwealth, it doesn't impose its will because it cannot, but by drawing the member states together under its diverse and multicultural umbrella it offers mutual support and advice. It isn't afraid to criticise as it did when taking the lead against South Africa's apartheid regime, but it will always do so in a spirit of wider understanding while urging conciliation. The Commonwealth largely stood behind Britain when, in 1982, it sent its forces to the Falklands to expel the Argentine invaders.

What is that ethos and why does it matter to Britain?

At its outset, despite the Imperial background, it was always assumed that the member states would enjoy increased levels of sovereignty with the declaration at the Imperial Conference in 1926 that all states were regarded as "autonomous communities within the British Empire, equal in status, in no way subordinate one to another in any aspect of the domestic or external affairs, though united by a common allegiance to the Crown, and freely associated as members of the British Commonwealth of Nations."

But the Commonwealth is so much more because it is a close-knit family with each nation sharing the same ideals and a sense of mutual caring of any united family. The Commonwealth is not powerful in the sense that it can brow beat others, but it is powerful in the sense that it is influential.

Sir Shridath "Sonny" Ramphal, Commonwealth Secretary General from 1975-1990, is remembered for saying while the Commonwealth can't negotiate, it can help the world to negotiate, and his own influence was highly regarded. Nelson Mandela said of him in 1990: "He is one of those men who have become famous because, in their fight for human justice, they have chosen the whole world as their theatre."

And that surely is the point of the Commonwealth. It has a unique ability to draw a third of the world's population together, and by the Commonwealth Charter adopted in 2013 its members are bound together sharing the same ambitious principles of democracy, freedom of expression and human rights.

Therefore, the answer to the first question is it relevant is absolutely. Democracy is a fragile concept, much admired but easily threatened. A majority vote is not always accepted as the final word even in nations where there is a freedom of expression. By signing up to the Commonwealth Charter, every member state pledges to aspire at least to its ideals. The free democratic vote in Great Britain to leave the European Union is still argued about and efforts are continually being made to overturn the decision, or at the very least disrupt what the Leave Campaign would portray as the benefits of Brexit. The "once on a lifetime vote" against an independent Scotland is still resisted. Equally, in the United States, the ousted president Donald Trump hotly disputed the outcome of the election declaring that his presidency was stolen from him in 2021. If arguably the two leading nations in the democratic world can have such "debates", all the more reason for having an organisation which embraces democratic values at its very heart.

It is relevant as whole nations like Ukraine, which sought the sanctuary of NATO membership when it came under attack from Russia, recognised the benefits of such solidarity. The Commonwealth nations don't offer the same military support as the NATO, but they do offer the chance to discuss at a high level both threats and opportunities.

In the same way, it is necessary because it encourages the high standards proclaimed in its Charter. Not everyone can reach those standards all the time, but it is a praiseworthy ambition. The Commonwealth is a forgiving organisation. Zimbabwe's membership was suspended in 2002 for breaches of international law under Robert Mugabe's presidency. He withdrew from the organisation the following year, but his successor, Emmerson Mnangagwa, in 2018 applied to re-join. As the Canadian Prime Minister, John Diefenbaker, said about South Africa's desire to return to the Commonwealth fold following its withdrawal in 1961, there would always be "a candle in the window" to welcome it back, which it did in 1994. Similarly, Pakistan left in 1972 and later re-joined in 1989, as did Fiji. Brunei and the Maldives did not immediately join the Commonwealth after declaring independence, but they did so 17 years later.

And if democracy is fragile so too is freedom of expression. It is nigh on impossible to speak one's mind about any topic today without causing offence to some group. What the Commonwealth Charter was no doubt more concerned about was free speech in terms of political expression and opposition to governments, but such are the sensitivities of so many people today that even the mildest comment or expression of opinion can cause outrage. However, it takes real courage to speak up in some authoritarian countries where the wrong word can mean a loss of liberty or worse.

The danger facing the Commonwealth comes in no small part from within the organisation itself. Questions are raised about how effective it is in policing its own ideals among the members, most notably human rights violations. But then the Commonwealth is not a policeman, it works by encouragement and example of others; it doesn't wave a big stick because it doesn't have one beyond suspending membership. Far better, it would argue, to encourage a member state to change it policies by persuasion than by threat. After all a country does not lose its authority by withdrawing its membership, but it does lose the ability to express its point of view at round tables such as the Commonwealth Heads of Government Meetings (CHOGM) every two years held in different member states.

The 2022 meeting, formally hosted by Prince Charles representing the Queen, was held in Rwanda, one of the more recent countries to join the association in 2009 and one with no ties to the British Empire; that same year English replaced French as the official language of higher education. The focus of the meeting, the first since the Pandemic, was on economic development, expanding intra-Commonwealth trade, youth development, tackling social equality, the impact of Covid-19 and climate action. Its theme was: "Delivering a common future: connecting, innovating, transforming." It is not widely known that CHOGM summits and other meetings, such as those of ministers, are the only kind of international gatherings where no interpreters are required, thanks to the English language that binds them together. (At the summit Gabon and Togo were admitted to the association.)

Addressing the question of some Commonwealth countries choosing to become republics, Prince Charles told leaders: "I want to say clearly, as I have said before, that each member's constitutional arrangement, as republic or monarchy, is purely a matter for each member country to decide." He added that it was a decision which can be made "calmly and without rancour." (*Sky News*, 24 June 2022)

As discussed, the "tradition" of the British monarch being Head of the Commonwealth is not compulsory or hereditary, and to some it may be too closely linked to Britain's colonial past. But that tradition will only last as long as its members chose to have the British monarch as their symbolic head. Perhaps it was convenient that Her Majesty the Queen had been monarch for so long. There was loyalty and respect over many decades and while Prince Charles was her designated successor, in all probability, he would remain head for his lifetime. However, the question is what is the glue which binds the Commonwealth together? Was it just Her Majesty or do the members feel there is real purpose in their close association?

It will depend on the leadership of future secretary generals but the benefits of close relations and understanding among so many countries is of paramount importance in a world which at times seems so fractious.

The Commonwealth is important for Great Britain, not in any proprietary sense because, like every other member state, it only has an equal voice. Marlborough House in London is its international headquarters but that is only because that is where it was launched. It is important because as Her Majesty so eloquently put it the Commonwealth was "an entirely new conception" and the loyalty she spoke of was a loyalty to one another not to her personally, at the same time proclaiming a desire for peace. It is a voluntary association encompassing every culture and religion, much as Britain is a country where every culture is welcomed, and every religion embraced. Britain is a focal point of the association without being a leader and, like Britain, it encourages trade links around the world. As the Queen said in her 2020 Commonwealth message: "Such a blend of traditions serves to make us stronger, individually and collectively, by providing the ingredients needed for social, political and economic resilience."

Britain, like every Commonwealth member, benefits economically by being part of the group. As Boris Johnson said prior to the 2022 CHOGM meeting in Rwanda: "It is an amazing fact that those invisible threads – particularly a common language and familiar legal and administrative systems – are of immense practical value for trade. Today the "Commonwealth advantage" knocks 21% off the cost of trade between members." (*Daily Telegraph*, 20 June 2022.)

It is worth considering what the world would be like without the Commonwealth, a unique body held together by tradition and without any formal obligation to one another. Gone would be the tradition of biennial meetings providing the opportunity to discuss mutual concerns and opportunities for trade. Gone would be the entities like the Commonwealth Africa Investment Fund which was established in 1996 to increase investment in Africa. Gone too would be numerous educational and cultural links between nations. And gone would be treasured sporting events like the Commonwealth Games.

Its longevity must reflect its value; an association of widely differing nations from across the globe which are able to come together to discuss in harmony the affairs of the world and reach a consensus. A consensus of opinion and approach to such matters as human rights and the environment. It may be a non-binding consensus because every member state must adapt their approach to domestic realities, but it is an ambition to reach the same goals.

What is clear is that the world would be the poorer without the Commonwealth of Nations because the world needs a unity of purpose to face the challenges of economics, politics and the environment. Unlike NATO there are no permanent members, no one has a veto, there are no byelaws to govern or restrict. Countries are members because they want to be and because they recognise the value of togetherness. No member is trying to control or influence the governance of another state, no member is more important or more influential than another. Prince William has even suggested that he doesn't expect to succeed his father as Head of the Commonwealth as of right when he becomes king.

The Commonwealth's value and importance is in its fundamental acceptance that all its members are equal regardless of size or length of membership and that membership is voluntary. No-one must join but they do even if there is no direct, historical connection to the Commonwealth or Empire; Mozambique, the former Portuguese colony, joined in 1995. The Commonwealth Foundation, which was established by the heads of government, in its own words "supports the belief that the Commonwealth is as much an association of peoples as it is of governments" and by learning from each other member states can build democratic societies.

As Head of the Commonwealth, Her Majesty had seen the association grow from just eight members to 56 and she has maintained that unity by more than 200 visits to every single Commonwealth country apart from Cameroon, which joined in 1995, and Rwanda.

Britain, therefore, recognises the value of such a diverse, multi-cultural gathering of nations and those members implicitly regard the Commonwealth as a valuable vehicle for international communication, diplomacy and trade.

Undoubtedly it was strengthened by the presence of the Queen for 70 years, but equally Britain holds the Commonwealth of Nations as a vital bulwark against conflict. If High Commissioners and heads of state can communicate openly as members of the same body with like-minded principles at its core, then peace can be maintained, trade can be conducted and economic growth, even among the smallest nation states, can flourish.

Our United Kingdom

"A Heritage to be Protected"

It may not be fashionable, it may sound a little boastful and therefore un-English, but perhaps it is time that we took just a little more pride in the all the riches we enjoy under the Crown in this truly fortunate realm, that makes up our United Kingdom.

Politicians will come and go, economies will boom and bust, even our cricket team will win some and lose some, but by and large we have much to be proud of, much to be thankful for and much to cherish.

We have been a United Kingdom since 1800 and, on the whole, we have prospered. We have changed but under one monarchy we have remained constant as one nation while all around us there has been turmoil. We have had good leaders, bold leaders, charismatic leaders and weak leaders, we have fought in many wars, we launched the Industrial Revolution, we have endured plagues, pandemics and economic hardship, but in the end the nation has survived. At the risk of adopting an ostrich's view of the world, the United Kingdom has fared at least as well, if not better, than many of its neighbours. We remain the financial services centre of Europe, if not the world, we have often been leaders in science, medical research, music and literature, and although relatively tiny in geographical size we still seem to be the fulcrum point as the world seesaws between economic crises and military threats, prosperity and peace.

People want to know where Great Britain stands if wars are declared, what our view might be when political upheaval affects countries anywhere in the world. Do we approve of a tough leader, or do we want to support their opponent? We have an important and permanent presence on the UN Security Council and are founder members of NATO, which in 2022 seemed to find a bolder voice and began bolstering its military position by increasing the strength of its rapid reaction force more than seven-fold to 300,000 troops, declaring Russia a "direct threat" to security.

Any fair audit of the United Kingdom's historical account must be positive. Despite the modern tendency to decry, or worse disregard, our past for fear of treading on sensitive toes, history shows that our united country's achievements are probably unique in this world, certainly for a nation of its size. We have earned the right to be proud and confident, while all the while retaining the British tendency for self-effacement.

We have remained a united nation for centuries, we have led the way in industry and science which have benefited every nation in the world. The industry, which in today's revisionist view is polluting our lives, helped millions to thrive, the literature and poetry, which today is forensically analysed for its politically incorrect content, is traduced and set aside instead of being appreciated for its lyrical beauty, and even our museums and art galleries which have illuminated the lives of generations are targeted by protestors at war with their sponsors instead of being carefully protected and admired. What is to be gained by gluing oneself to a masterpiece work of art which then needs to be restored? (Constable's masterpiece The Hay Wain damaged by Just stop Oil protest – *Daily Telegraph* 5 July 2022)

No-one pretends that our history is without blemish, we were one of the greatest sea faring nations and once had the biggest navy in the world which helped our nation and, yes, our empire grow. But there were also pirates and privateers, there were slave traders and there was abuse. The question remains how should we treat our history? Should we focus exclusively on the negative side of our balance sheet because it has been ignored for too long, or should we address it, learn from it, while acknowledging its flaws? The modern trend is for nationwide self-flagellation. We are ashamed of our past mistakes while air-brushing our achievements. We are constantly comparing ourselves with other nations seeking to admire their achievements while denigrating our own.

Critics, particularly of governments, take a short-term view. It is the job of the opposition parties to try and discredit every policy and attack every initiative, it is their job because they want to get into power themselves. But this book takes the long view.

What can be gained by fragmenting the United Kingdom, which has stood the test of time, into even smaller nations without financial, political or military influence or standing? How many times should we vote before accepting the verdict of the general population? The country may at times be buffeted by powerful economic headwinds which opponents can reasonably claim they could handle better without having to say precisely what they would do differently; it may be threatened by wars, it may suffer from epidemics, it may even lose its prime ministers mid-term, but these are all the events which can beset any administration. If they are mishandled, we can vote the governments out of office; but can one believe that a fragmented nation would work, that what would in effect be an outcrop of a former United Kingdom in the north or the west of the country would fare any better? How would they be financed? How would they trade with the country they chose to leave behind or the rest of the world? How would they defend themselves in time of war? When Commonwealth countries voted to become republics and appoint their own heads of state replacing the Queen, they all realised that they would benefit by remaining part of a larger grouping, gaining strength from trading ties and political friendship rather than striking out on their own. Why then did the UK vote to leave the European Union some might ask? The answer the Brexiteers would give is that Brussels was exceeding its original economic mandate and exerting too much control over the sovereign authority of the British parliament and courts. The Remainers, who smelled blood with the toppling of Boris Johnson in July 2022, were convinced that Brexit was a terrible mistake which had to be reversed.

No-one stops to consider what their duty is before making their demands for rights and benefits. It is what one might call the free buffet syndrome where one can eat and drink as much as one likes because it is there and if one doesn't feast on it, someone else will. When suddenly there is a shortage, then the complaints start once the stampede to grab as much as possible has subsided. It applies to many sectors: where is the ambulance one called for hours ago – it is dealing with other patients, some more deserving or needy than others. Was it necessary for the motorcyclist to speed and lose control injuring themselves or others in a crash, could that obese person not have stopped bingeing on poor food before collapsing with a heart attack? It applies to landowners who are eager to jump on the demand for new houses and apply for planning permission regardless of the impact on local infrastructure and its ability to cope with the population increase, or the countryside. It applied during the Coronavirus pandemic when many, possibly thousands, jumped on the furlough scheme to boost their incomes when it became evident later that they were not entitled to a penny. Of course, it should have been more closely monitored but the government, like every government around the world, was fighting multiple fires just to get on top of the outbreak.

Perhaps it is human nature always to be taking rather than holding back, perhaps we really do just take our riches for granted. But rather than complain when the queues in A&E seem to get ever longer, we need to be thankful for the fact that we have a queue to join in the first place with guaranteed treatment at the end of it.

While the population continues to grow there will be more mouths to feed, more demand for housing, schooling and GP services, which for now at least the United Kingdom can provide. If we take care of our land, we can grow more food and raise more livestock but that comes with responsibility. It means that instead of feasting on the free buffet of imported produce we shop locally and support our farmers, it means fewer protests against technology designed to improve yields safely, it means more respect for our countryside, less waste, less litter, less impatience on country roads as the tractors make their way to the next field.

To preserve our nation which continues to attract visitors from around the world we must protect our heritage and proclaim our history proudly. It is the whole of our past which makes us the united nation that we are today. Just as much as we should protect the beauty of this green and pleasant land, we need to protect our historical buildings and the cityscapes of London, Bristol, Oxford and Edinburgh and so many more. We need to take pride in our own smaller towns and villages because they were there before us and will be there when we have gone.

To build for the future of our nation will undoubtedly mean more restraint and more personal responsibility. We will need more houses, but developments will have to come with an infrastructure to match: schools, GP surgeries and hospitals. In the meantime, to cope with the growth there will have to be less feasting at the free buffet that the United Kingdom has become. Water as we have noted (Chapter 11) is already a precious resource and one which should not be squandered. We need more reservoirs and fewer leaking pipes. Our rivers, seas and the oceans around us are every bit as valuable as any treasure and it is our responsibility to protect them. Although anecdotal evidence suggests litter on our beaches is falling, 75% of what is recovered is either plastic or polystyrene, and cases of children being burned on buried portable barbecues are still reported, not to mention the insanity of having a barbecue on tinder dry land in times of a drought sparking uncontrollable fires.

Our United Kingdom is a land of opportunity for all regardless of background upbringing or ethnicity. The only requirement is hard work. Nadhim Zahawi who briefly became Chancellor of the Exchequer in July 2022, arrived in the country aged 11 when his family fled Iraq speaking no English. He was to be followed only months later by Rishi Sunak becoming the country's first British-Asian prime minister. There are no barriers to success. Our hospitals are full of consultants, surgeons and nurses whose family history can be traced to overseas lands, they are welcomed as much as they are needed. Our banks and businesses are led by men and women of every heritage because they are the best in their field, and our universities are full of students and professors of every nationality eager to learn and to teach. Nothing is off the curriculum; nothing is too sensitive to be debated and nothing should be. If we want to learn from past mistakes they need to be studied as much as the greatest achievements. To ban books because of their perceived bias is as dangerous as *Kristallnacht* and the best of our teachers are resisting this drive towards sanitising our studies lest they cause offence. To give "trigger point" warnings about Shakespeare plays because they contain misogynistic, racist or violent content is as ridiculous as it sounds. Education demands that we learn about the British Empire not because it was without fault but because of the impact it had on so many, its achievements and its errors.

This freedom of study and expression is a hallmark of British life despite the concerted efforts of extremists to the contrary. There is a long way to go before even Britain can claim to be a truly multi-cultural society. There is a long way to go before every citizen can be lifted out of poverty and every child guaranteed a safe and secure upbringing, but there are opportunities for everyone to climb whatever ladder they choose in business, in sport, in politics or religion. Nowhere is off-limits as the glass ceilings are, one by one, being shattered.

The choice for anyone in the United Kingdom is there for everyone whether they are born and bred here or newly arrived immigrants, if they are prepared to make the effort and seize their chances. In 2021 23 million people claimed benefits of which 9.9 million were of working age. (www.gov.uk). Meanwhile there were a record number of 1.3 million job vacancies in the three months to May 2022, more than half a million compared with the same period in 2021. One can get qualified or even learn the English language and achieve one's wildest dreams because there are no restrictions on ambition – even to becoming Chancellor of the Exchequer.

The danger, of course, is that we take the largesse of free benefits, free education, free health service for granted because we know that without lifting a finger the support will always be there. No-one counts how many children a mother has; no-one asks how she expects to care for them because she has that freedom of choice. In A&E there may be light questioning about someone's lifestyle which contributed to an illness, but no one is refused treatment because that is their right, just join the long queue and wait your turn.

Our United Kingdom is as benign as our climate, even if occasionally the storms break, a pandemic strikes, the economy struggles or the NHS looks close to buckling under the strain of ever-increasing demands. It is resilient as well as benign. It can withstand political turmoil, it can vote out governments and overthrow prime ministers without violent bloodshed above all it tends to look for compromise even if the tone of political debate in the 21st century is less polite. The manoeuvrings of politicians can be a devious as the Medicis of Florence in the 15th century, but when the dust settles, life for the average person has a way of carrying on and making do, as very often they barely take time to glance up from their labours to notice what is happening in Westminster. That speaks to the resilience of the British people and their innate common-sense and practicality. If there is nothing they can do about a situation, at least until the next general election, they will keep calm and carry on.

The foundations of the United Kingdom, built over centuries, are what will protect it in the future. Few foresaw the political chaos which developed in the summer of 2022, but the system ensured that the government of the nation would continue. A large majority for a government was no guarantee of clinging on to power as Boris Johnson and before him, Theresa May and Tony Blair discovered. The fickle whims of a volatile electorate and their own party colleagues proved too much. However, when new leaders were appointed the day-to-day business of government resumed, as it always does.

It is the good nature of the British character which always wins through, and it is the fundamental innate wisdom of the ordinary citizen which prevents the country from lurching too violently to any extreme; middle of the road may sound dull, but it protects the country from false prophets. There are those on the left of centre who would welcome a return to extreme socialism where the formerly powerful trade unions held the country to ransom. Equally there are those who yearn for the no-nonsense almost dictatorial politics of Thatcherism which broke the union stranglehold, and the economic equilibrium was restored. Invariably history tells us that the great British compromise triumphs in the end.

Great Britain loves their eccentrics and what they call charismatic characters. Boris Johnson was one of those, leading the country and the Conservative Party to a huge majority in the 2019 election. But in July 2022 his own party forced him out of office, the "herd" as Boris called them in his uncompromising resignation speech on the steps of 10 Downing Street, had moved against him, his tendency to play fast and loose with the rules, if not the truth, had cost him his premiership prematurely. The commentators said he was his own worst enemy and it was time, people suggested, for a safer pair of hands, if not dull certainly less eccentric. The clever repartee, the erudite witticisms could be put away, the focus was on reviving the economy with practical solutions. It made for a duller debate, but the British people wanted to dial down the rhetoric, while of course the opposition wanted a new government.

Away from the drama, the United Kingdom ploughs a steady course, exemplified by the serenity of Her Majesty who watched benevolently on as new prime ministers presented themselves at her door, each one politely discussing anything but politics, Her Majesty wondering how many more she was likely to meet during her reign because, of course, she has seen it all before. Like her own horses, she had winners and losers, and she took the political highs and lows of her realm in her stride, the only difference being she had cheered her own equine winners to the roof tops, her prime ministers she had just cordially wished them well.

Our United Kingdom, therefore, is indeed a blessed isle, a leader among nations of greater size but less standing. Our country which welcomes honest endeavour but will resist the freeloaders. It is prepared to stand shoulder to shoulder with its allies to fight for what is right and not be scared to speak out against the aggressor. When China pressed it ambitions too aggressively representing the "biggest long-term threat to our economic and national security" it was called out by the head of MI5, Ken McCallum, and counterpart at the FBI, Christopher Wray. Mr McCallum said MI5 was doubling its work against Chinese activity. (*BBC*, 7 July 2022).

By not being afraid to stand up for what is right, the United Kingdom makes itself a target from individuals as well as nations. Mr McCallum said: "MI5's counter-terrorist work remains intense. Syria, Somalia and Afghanistan continue to generate threats. Our most immediate UK challenge is lone terrorists – Islamist extremist and right-wing extremist – radicalised online, acting at pace, in unpredictable ways." (*www.mI5.gov.uk*).

We are, nevertheless, blessed by good fortune, by our natural surroundings, by our historical buildings, by our inventiveness, by our scientists, our engineers, our artists. The list is endless, and it is that which attracts so many to our shores. Somehow it was all encapsulated by the millions who thronged the Mall in London to mark the Queen's Platinum Jubilee in 2022. All rancour, all concerns were swept aside for just a few days as visitors from around the world joined British citizens in celebration of 70 years of service – a unique event to honour a unique achievement which will never be matched by any other leader in any other country.

This is the country which through its unparalleled achievements has both bestrode the globe and led it in wartime and peace. It has triumphed in adversity and shown compassion in victory. It has brought education to the world and been equally eager to learn from others. Despite siren voices to the contrary, it is prepared to acknowledge its shortcomings and always be prepared to learn from its mistakes.

As the world moved into the middle of the 21st century, the United Kingdom was at the vanguard of new initiatives, innovative technologies, a leader in diplomatic efforts to find peaceful solutions to the troubles around the globe and always ready to lend its support to the downtrodden and oppressed. These are the attributes which make a great nation, which should never again be taken for granted, a United Kingdom.

Epilogue

Finally, after 70 years of unswerving duty, Her Majesty died on 8 September 2022 at her favourite home, Balmoral in Aberdeenshire surrounded by her family. To the end she had made it clear that her focus would be on inspiring "unity and national identity." (*Daily Telegraph,* 3 July 2022). Such words were not used lightly, and one suspects the emphasis was on the word "unity". No other person, no other monarch, had done more to demonstrate the value of dedication to her realm, to be prepared to work tirelessly even on her holidays, and never to have faltered in her affection and devotion to her people. She did indeed dedicate her life to serve us as she promised on her 21st birthday in 1947: "I declare before you all that my whole life whether it be long or short shall be devoted to your service and the service of our great imperial family to which we all belong."

The death of Her Majesty sparked renewed anti-monarchy mumblings on social media and some solitary placards in the street – "Make Elizabeth the last"- but it was cautious and low key, running as it did against the tide of emotion that swept the country. What was missing in their arguments was an alternative proposal. They wanted to open the debate without declaring how they would replace the monarchy which for centuries has served the nation well and provided a unifying point where politics divided, and politicians failed. There was an inevitability about the campaign, suddenly released from 70 years of virtual silence, but it still lacked the force of sound argument, instead engaging in disrespectful rhetoric. It will find a new, louder voice just as King Charles, by contrast, must now choose his words carefully as monarch and seeks to forge his own way mindful of the traps and pitfalls which will be laid in his path.

The sudden resignation announcement of Prime Minister Johnson in July 2022 somehow made unity an important word. Eleven candidates immediately put themselves forward as potential successors, each one saying how they would manage the affairs of the nation so much better than the man they had served under, and more effectively than the rest of the other candidates. In short order that was whittled down to two and eventually the Conservative Party members voted for Liz Truss as party leader and prime minister, who promised to "deliver, deliver, deliver" on her daunting in-tray and confident that

"We can ride out the storm" – a storm that was to gather strength following the mini-budget on 23 September 2022 which contributed to turmoil in the financial markets, the rapid dismissal of her Chancellor, Kwasi Kwarteng, after just 38 days, the resignation of the newly appointed Home Secretary, Suella Braverman, and even threats to Liz Truss's own position as she apologised to the nation for trying to go "too far, too fast" in her ambition for growth. However, it wasn't enough and Liz Truss herself announced her resignation as Conservative leader and prime minister on 20 October, formally handing over power on 25 October after 49 days in office.

But that storm was still to break, meanwhile no-one begrudged Her Majesty's breaking with the tradition of her reign by accepting the resignation of Boris Johnson as prime minister and inviting his successor to form a government while on her summer break at Balmoral rather than travelling back to London and conducting the ceremony at Buckingham Palace. It was to be her last formal act carried out with her beaming smile just 48 hours before her death.

The Scottish First Minister, Nicola Sturgeon, took the opportunity of the Conservative leadership campaign to announce that she would push for a second independence referendum in 2023 saying that whoever won the Conservative party leadership contest would be "another prime minster

Scotland hasn't voted for." (*Daily Mail*, 14 July 2022). But that was never the 'unity and national identity' Her Majesty had been urging. Take pride in being a Scot or a Welshman but not to the extent that you would want to tear the nation apart for some fleeting political whim or even obsession. In his parting shots to Parliament, Boris Johnson gave his successor these words of advice from the Dispatch Box on 20 July 2022: "Number one: stay close to the Americans, stick up for the Ukrainians, stick up for freedom and democracy everywhere. Cut taxes and deregulate wherever you can to make this the greatest place to live and invest, which it is." Later, when he visited Kyiv to mark Ukraine's independence day on 24 August 2022, Johnson urged the west to stay the course: "We also know that if we're paying in our energy bills for the evils of Vladimir Putin, the people of Ukraine are paying in their blood."

While the turmoil in government continued during those summer months, the key foundations of our United Kingdom became evermore important. At our head we had the Queen and her heirs, rock like and imperturbable as the infighting and opposition attacks continued until the next general election was to be called.

All the while there was a war going on in Ukraine which was drawing in support from around the western world. Britain's Defence Secretary, Ben Wallace, was one member of

Johnson's cabinet not to resign or enter the leadership contest, saying: "My focus is on my current job and keeping this great country safe." (*Guardian*, 9 July 2022) In the (first) cabinet reshuffle which followed Liz Truss's appointment he kept his job. It remained to be seen, however, whether pledges from various leadership contenders to increase the strength of the British military would be delivered on the battlefield when the brutal reality of the country's finances were considered, and all departments were forced to rein in their expenditure. Nevertheless, the military's role and commitment in conflicts and natural disasters are world renowned and could never be taken for granted.

The economic impact of the Russian invasion of Ukraine was increasing in the summer of 2022 and the long-term fallout was bound to be severe, although the first signs that Putin's forces would not be able to sustain the onslaught began to be seen as western supplied technology and weapons proved to be effective.

But the standards the UK aspired to in so many walks of life remained inviolable. Somehow the NHS would continue to serve all-comers regardless of wealth or origin, particularly if we did more to help ourselves keep healthy. Somehow our schools and universities would continue to educate to the highest standards despite challenges to freedom of speech, producing world renowned scholars, scientists, engineers and writers, and somehow our police force would continue to serve. And despite the political upheaval which led to the resignation of Prime Minister Johnson and the financial chaos of the Truss government's few weeks in office and her own resignation, our democracy would prevail. In time it would find new leaders of calibre, character and charisma to ensure the unity and national identity of the country remained intact; a far cry from the riots and political upheaval in places like Sri Lanka that same summer which forced President Gotabaya Rajapaksa to flee his country as protestors stormed the presidential palace.

As a nation we have much to be thankful for and little to complain about because we have a welfare system to protect the least well off and an economy which can withstand the worst crises. At the time of writing there were jobs for those who wanted to work and were physically able, there was an immigration policy which encouraged the brightest and the best to work and study here, and a determined policy to deter illegal immigration. However, in the summer of 2022, the cost-of-living pressures brought on in no small part by the war in Ukraine, were tough for many, there were multiple strikes in pursuit of higher wages as inflation started to rise, there were staff shortages in key industries, there was still the residual threat from Covid 19 and disarray in politics. This was the in-basket awaiting the country's new leader as the post changed hands in rapid succession. Liz Truss was succeeded by Rishi Sunak as the Conservative "unity" candidate in a quick-fire election lasting just over a week in October 2022, making him the third prime minister in seven weeks and, aged 42, the youngest leader in 200 years.

But we also have a sound democracy developed over centuries, a professional and well-armed military to defend us, a health service always ready to heal us, an education system which can carry the able and the willing to the highest levels in business, medicine, politics and the arts, and a police force prepared to face any danger to protect us.

If we compare our good fortune honestly, the United Kingdom is indeed a fortunate country, a tolerant land prepared to welcome all who are equally prepared to work hard to achieve their own dreams.

For seventy years we were privileged to have a head of state who was revered by the world and its leaders. As she lay in state in Westminster Hall hundreds of thousands waited round the clock in five-mile-long queues for days to pay their final respects, and millions around the world watched on television. On Monday 19 September, with faultless precision, the combined armed forces, as well as overseas contingents, carried Her Majesty first to Westminster Abbey for her funeral service attended by a congregation of some two thousand, including 100 heads of state, 500 delegations, and individuals who had served the Queen in capacities great and small throughout her life. From the abbey she made her way passed crowds, sometimes twenty deep, along the road to Windsor Castle for a more intimate committal service held at St George's Chapel. Once again, the crowds in their thousands lined the Long Walk up to the castle, some quietly applauding, others shedding tears, as the cortège marched slowly by, passing in a poignant tribute Emma, the pony the Queen used to ride standing alongside her head groom, Terry Pendry, and waiting for her arrival her two corgis, Sandy and Muick. Finally, at the closure of the service, His Majesty King Charles placed the Queen's Company Camp Colour of the Grenadier Guards on her coffin, the orb, sceptre, and crown were placed on the high altar and the Lord Chamberlain symbolically broke his Wand of Office in two, and then Her Majesty was at last laid to rest beside her late husband, the Duke of Edinburgh, as her personal piper played a last lament.

In truth we have little to complain about when we look at the rest of the world and yet we still take it all for granted. Well, never again.

Postscript

As a New Year dawned there was a chance to reflect in January 2023 on what Great Britain had achieved, what it hoped for and what it could and should be proud of amid the challenges it faced.

So much of life had been dominated by the Russian invasion of Ukraine which had thrown the energy and financial markets into turmoil, while never forgetting the suffering and courage of the Ukrainian people themselves. Great Britain had taken the lead in Europe throwing its political and military support behind the resistance, standing alongside the United States. As the winter of 2022 took hold, the world in turn held its breath to see if Putin's forces could be repelled once and for all when Spring broke, as his supporters (China and India) turned lukewarm.

Domestically, Britain faced its own challenges. The NHS, buckling under the strains of stubborn Covid cases combined with winter flu, faced widespread strike action. No-one doubted the workload faced by staff and their resilience, but while the service needed reform the government, nevertheless, had to find a way to balance the books. There was industrial action, it seemed, every day of the week as the year came to a close: the railways, postal workers, Border Force staff and teachers. Inflation had peaked but remained high and families were struggling as the cost of living hit them hard. The military had to step in, as they always do, to plug the gaps: driving ambulances and manning passport control.

But there were self-inflicted injuries which were doing their best to tear at the fabric of the nation.

The woke agenda had spread like its own virus infecting every walk of life from business to entertainment, education to politics. But there were signs of resistance. When TV programmes showed a historical bias, it was picked up. When once impartial news programmes strayed with an anti-government slant, they were challenged. When universities feared to allow free speech, they were roundly criticised, but not before lecturers were forced from their posts. But where there was a deafening silence was in defence of the monarchy which increasingly seemed to be coming under attack from within as well as without.

Britain is a land of free speech, a country where you are allowed to express an opinion without fear of attack, verbally and physically. It is also a land of tolerance and respect, or should be. It comes down to good manners which may sound old fashioned, but it is at the heart of diplomacy. It allows hostile nations to conduct business, and it should enable different generations at a personal level, different ethnic groups, indeed all people to behave in a civilised manner without resorting to argument and even violence.

The death of HM Queen Elizabeth united a nation and countless millions around the world in both sorrow and respect. The most recognised global figure succeeded in her long life and reign in providing an example for all to follow. Her life was not without heartache, but she chose to channel her sorrow in such a way that no blame was ever attached. She never gave an interview, choosing always to keep her counsel. She undoubtedly held strong opinions, but even in her private audiences with 15 British prime ministers, they would surely have been tempered by gentle advice born out of 70 years of experience.

The Royal Family, thanks to Her Majesty's long reign, has served the nation well and with the coronation of King Charles 111 on 6 May 2023, it remains steady. Brickbats may be thrown from the side-lines, but the enduring nature of the line of succession means even the most scurrilous attacks, which can never be publicly defended, will have no lasting impact. Never complain, never explain, the family motto, is the surest defence.

Under King Charles's guidance the monarchy will adapt and modernise. It will be a slimmed down institution with the focus on fewer working royal members as befits the modern age. As the late Prince Philip would have advised: Keep it simple and let's get on with it. However, a downsized monarchy should not be one without splendour and a degree of pomp as King Charles wanted at his coronation – the magic and the mystique of royalty must be preserved because of the vital role the monarchy plays in our constitution.

The whole world will be watching to see how the new Carolean Age will unfold. It is an age full of challenges, political, economic and personal, but thanks to the solid and evolving foundations of our monarchy there would always be a constancy, an unbreakable thread running through its core. It is the nation's reliability over centuries which has proved to be an attraction to countless visitors, immigrants and investors. It has a history without parallel, it accepts its historical flaws unflinchingly and has learned from them. It is a nation where people want to launch their businesses and raise their families because of the freedoms we have long enjoyed.

The future will undoubtedly be dominated by inspiring technological invention and Britain will be at the forefront of that change, always ready to adapt and evolve. HM King Charles was himself a pioneer when it came to climate change and the environment, and in his new, burdensome role he will seek to help the monarchy meet all the challenges which lie ahead.

About the Authors

Bob Whittington is a former journalist in newspapers, BBC Radio and Television, and ITN. He is an author and ghost writer. His books include: In the Shadow of Power and Money Talks (Whittles Publishing).

Professor Kartar Lalvani OBE PhD, DSc Bonn, FRPharmS London is the founder and chairman of the Britain's No 1 vitamin company, Vitabiotics Ltd, and author of The Making of India - The Untold Story of British Enterprise (Bloomsbury Publishing). Professor Lalvani graduated in Pharmacy at King's College London under Prof Arnold Beckett and moved to the University of Bonn for advanced studies in Pharmaceutical Science obtaining a DSc with Distinction. An honorary professor at Université de Franche-Comté, Besançon, France, Professor Lalvani is a practising Sikh, a philanthropist, private scholar and historian.

Photo Credits

King Charles III

Title: Charles, Prince of Wales in Jersey on 18 July 2012.

Author: Dan Marsh

Source:

https://www.flickr.com/photos/30692593@N07/7597030944

Licence: Creative Commons — Attribution-ShareAlike 2.0 Generic — CC BY-SA 2.0

Queen Camilla

Title: Duchess of Cornwall, Duchess of Cambridge & Prince Harry at Trooping the Colour, London, 16 June 2012

Author: Carfax2, derivative work: Tktru

Source: Derived from above titled work

Licence: Creative Commons — Attribution-ShareAlike 3.0 Unported — CC BY-SA 3.0

Queen Elizabeth II

Title: Queen Elizabeth II greets NASA GSTC employees, May 8, 2007

Author: NASA/Bill Ingalls

Source: NASA - The Queen Walks to Building 8

Ingram Content Group UK Ltd.
Milton Keynes UK
UKHW020630100523
421517UK00014B/295

9 781916 540750